D1055499

#1 JOP AND BLIP WANNA KNOW

CAN YOU HEAR A PENGUIN FART ON MARS?

AND OTHER EXCELLENT QUESTIONS

JIM BENTON

#1

JOP AND BLIP WANNA KNOW

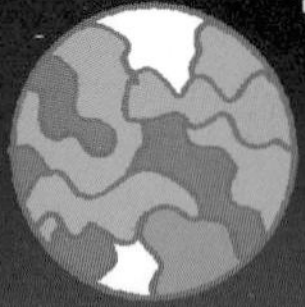

HARPER alley
An Imprint of HarperCollinsPublishers

TO ALL THE SCIENTISTS WHO WORK SO HARD TO HELP US.

HARPERALLEY IS AN IMPRINT OF HARPERCOLLINS PUBLISHERS.

JOP AND BLIP WANNA KNOW #1: CAN YOU HEAR A PENGUIN FART ON MARS?
COPYRIGHT © 2021 BY JIM BENTON
ALL RIGHTS RESERVED. PRINTED IN BOSNIA AND HERZEGOVINA.
NO PART OF THIS BOOK MAY BE USED OR REPRODUCED IN ANY MANNER WHATSOEVER WITHOUT
WRITTEN PERMISSION EXCEPT IN THE CASE OF BRIEF QUOTATIONS EMBODIED IN CRITICAL ARTICLES
AND REVIEWS. FOR INFORMATION ADDRESS HARPERCOLLINS CHILDREN'S BOOKS, A DIVISION OF
HARPERCOLLINS PUBLISHERS, 195 BROADWAY, NEW YORK, NY 10007.
WWW.HARPERALLEY.COM

LIBRARY OF CONGRESS CONTROL NUMBER: 2020947267
ISBN 978-0-06-297292-7 — ISBN 978-0-06-297293-4 (PBK.)

DRAWN WITH A FLAIR PEN ON CHEAP PAPER AND COLORED IN PHOTOSHOP.
TYPOGRAPHY BY JIM BENTON AND ERICA DE CHAVEZ
21 22 23 24 25   GPS   10 9 8 7 6 5 4 3 2 1
❖
FIRST EDITION

TABLE OF CONTENTS

THE PENGUIN PUZZLE

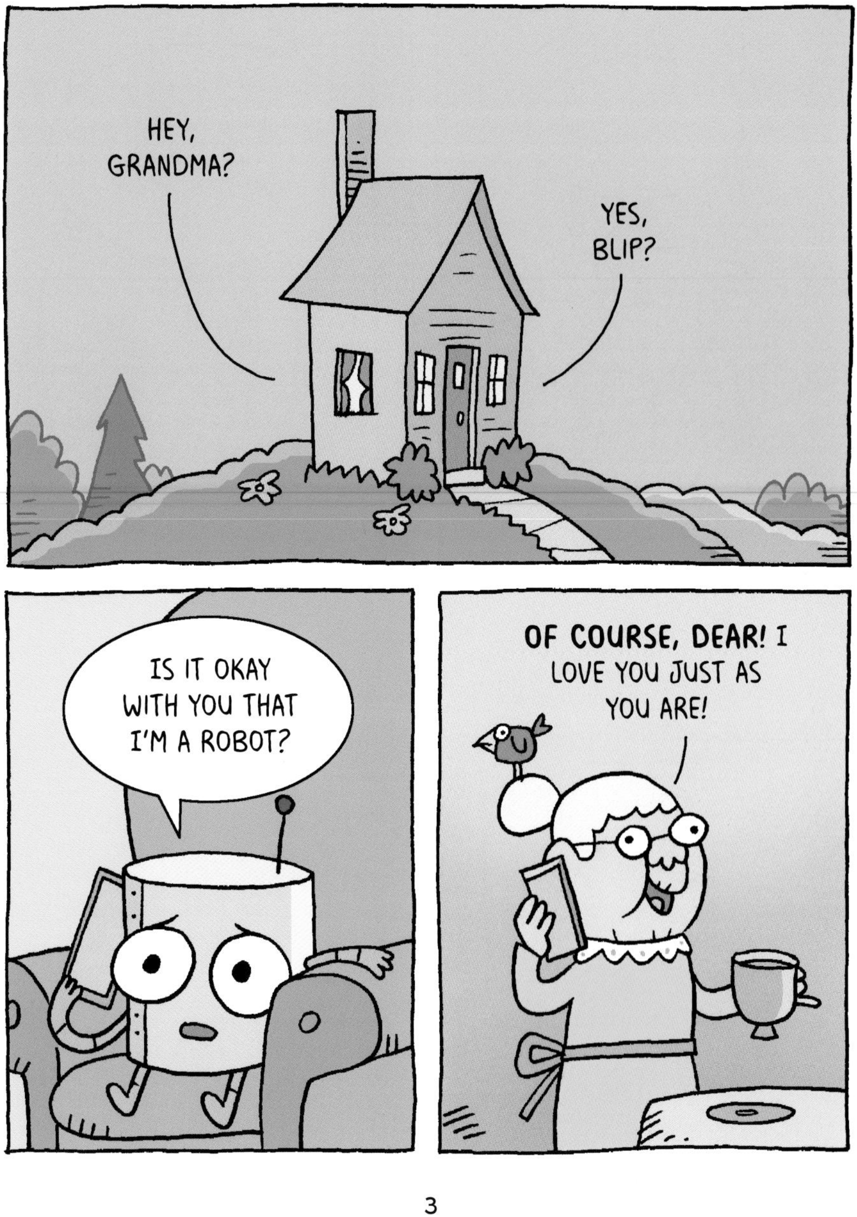
HEY, GRANDMA?
YES, BLIP?
IS IT OKAY WITH YOU THAT I'M A ROBOT?
OF COURSE, DEAR! I LOVE YOU JUST AS YOU ARE!

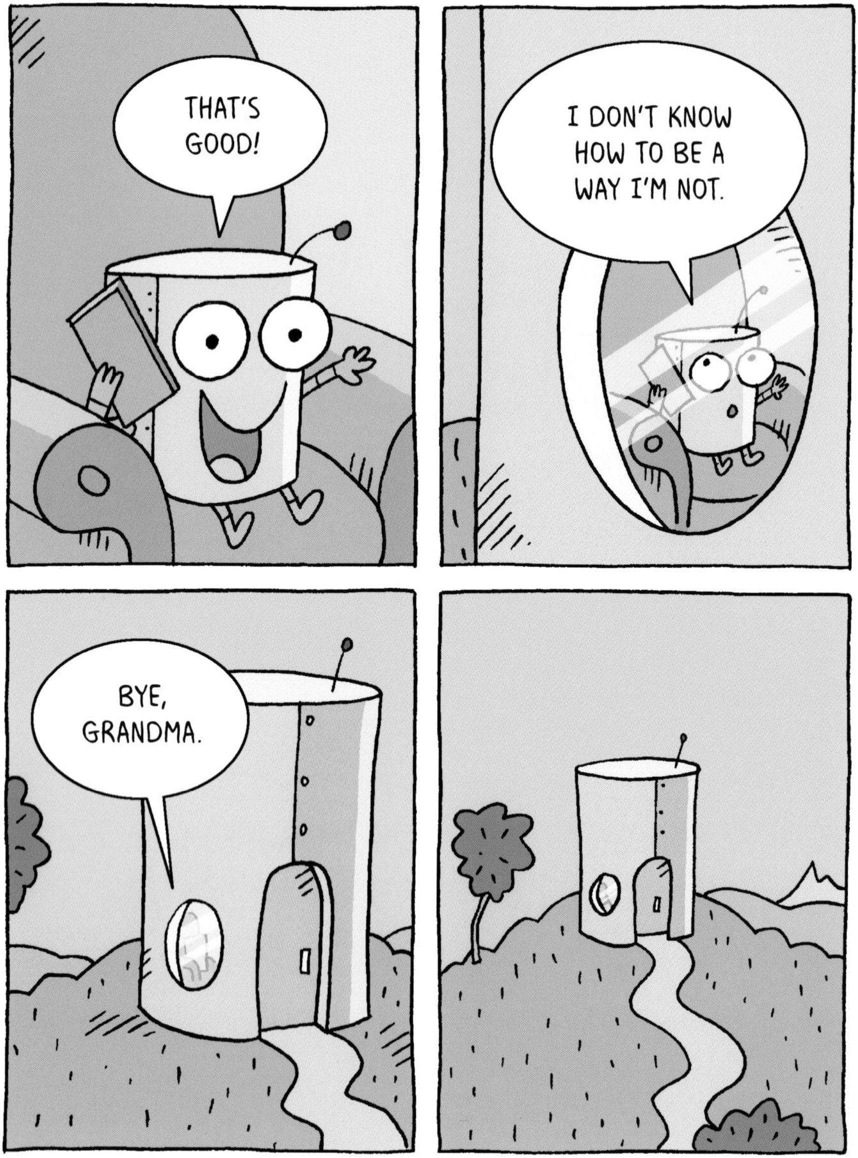
THAT'S GOOD!
I DON'T KNOW HOW TO BE A WAY I'M NOT.
BYE, GRANDMA.

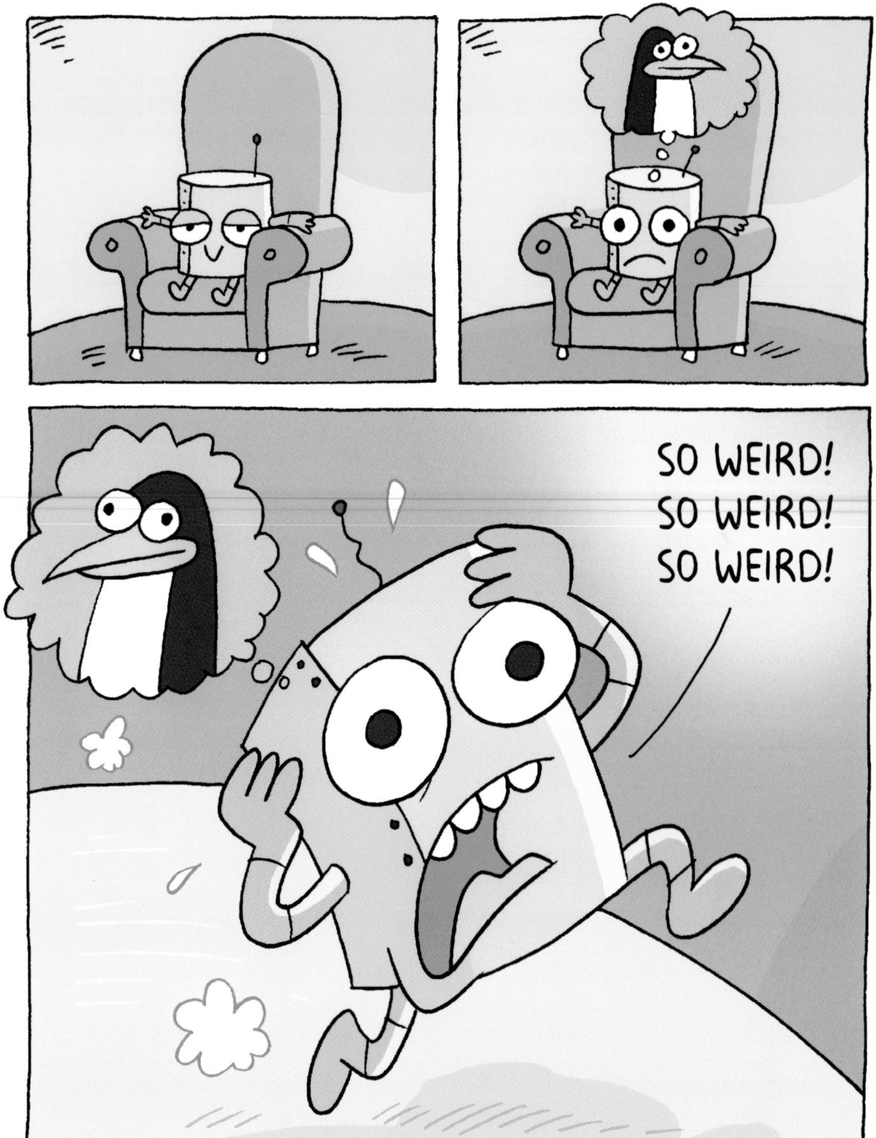
SO WEIRD!
SO WEIRD!
SO WEIRD!

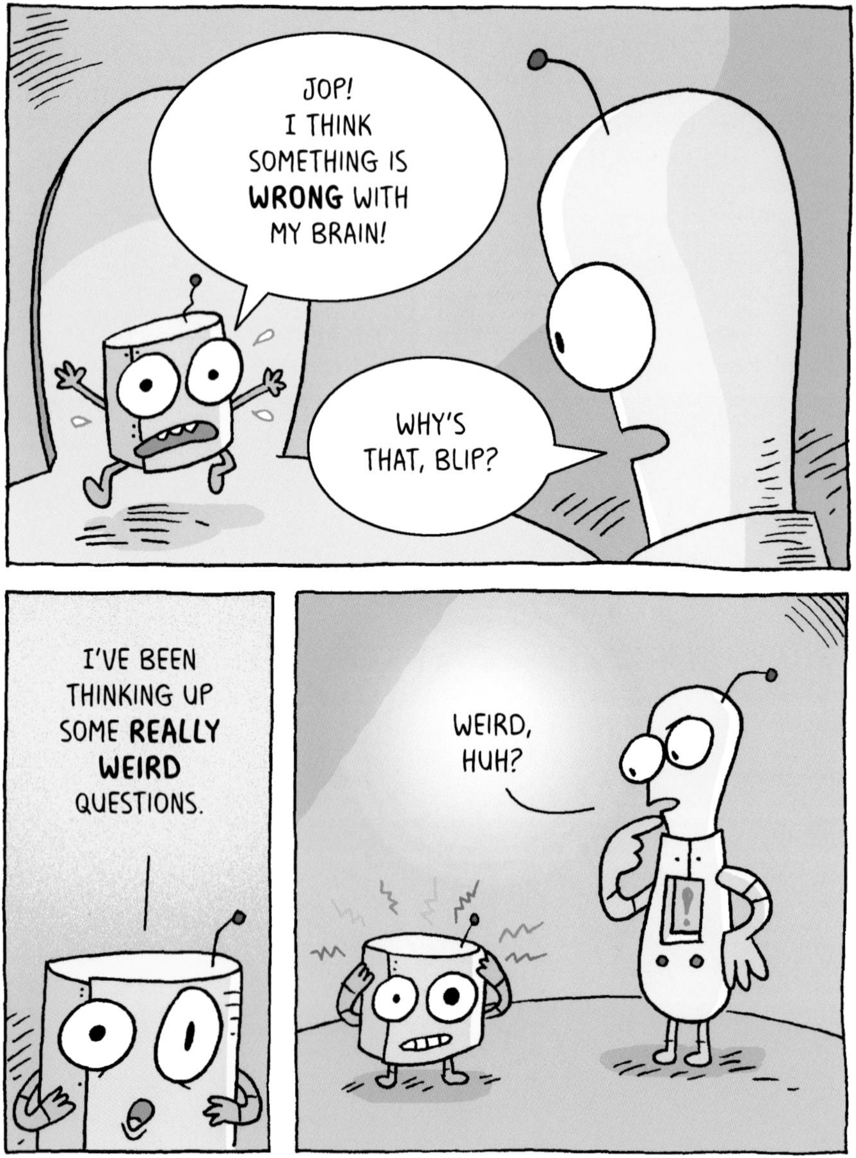
JOP! I THINK SOMETHING IS **WRONG** WITH MY BRAIN!
WHY'S THAT, BLIP?
I'VE BEEN THINKING UP SOME **REALLY WEIRD** QUESTIONS.
WEIRD, HUH?

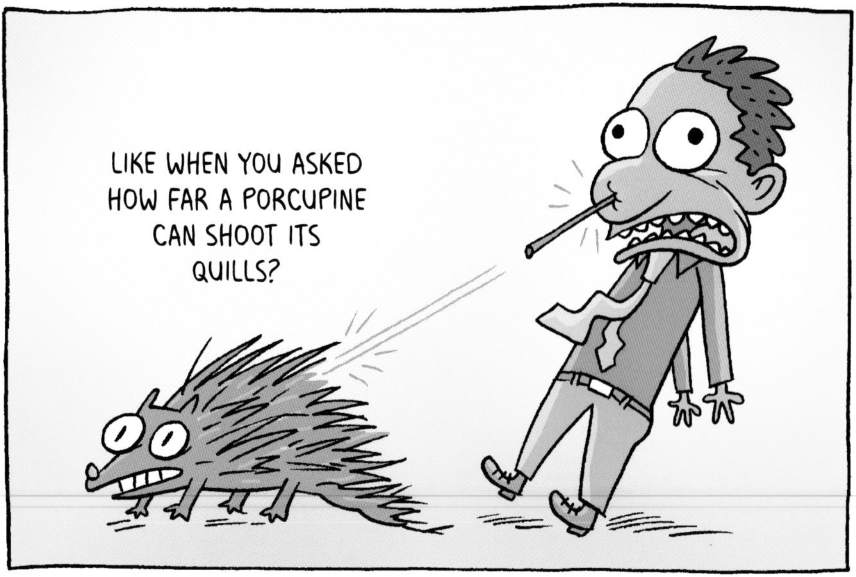
LIKE WHEN YOU ASKED HOW FAR A PORCUPINE CAN SHOOT ITS QUILLS?

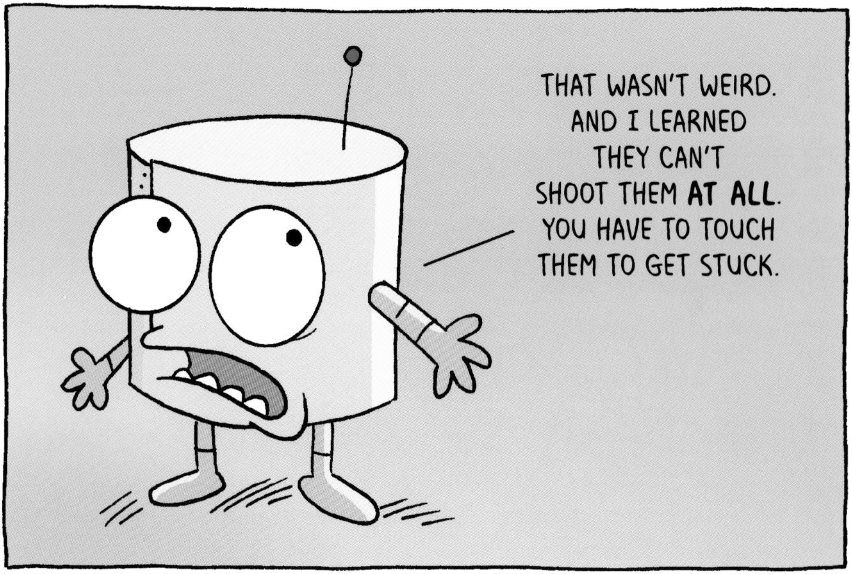
THAT WASN'T WEIRD. AND I LEARNED THEY CAN'T SHOOT THEM **AT ALL**. YOU HAVE TO TOUCH THEM TO GET STUCK.

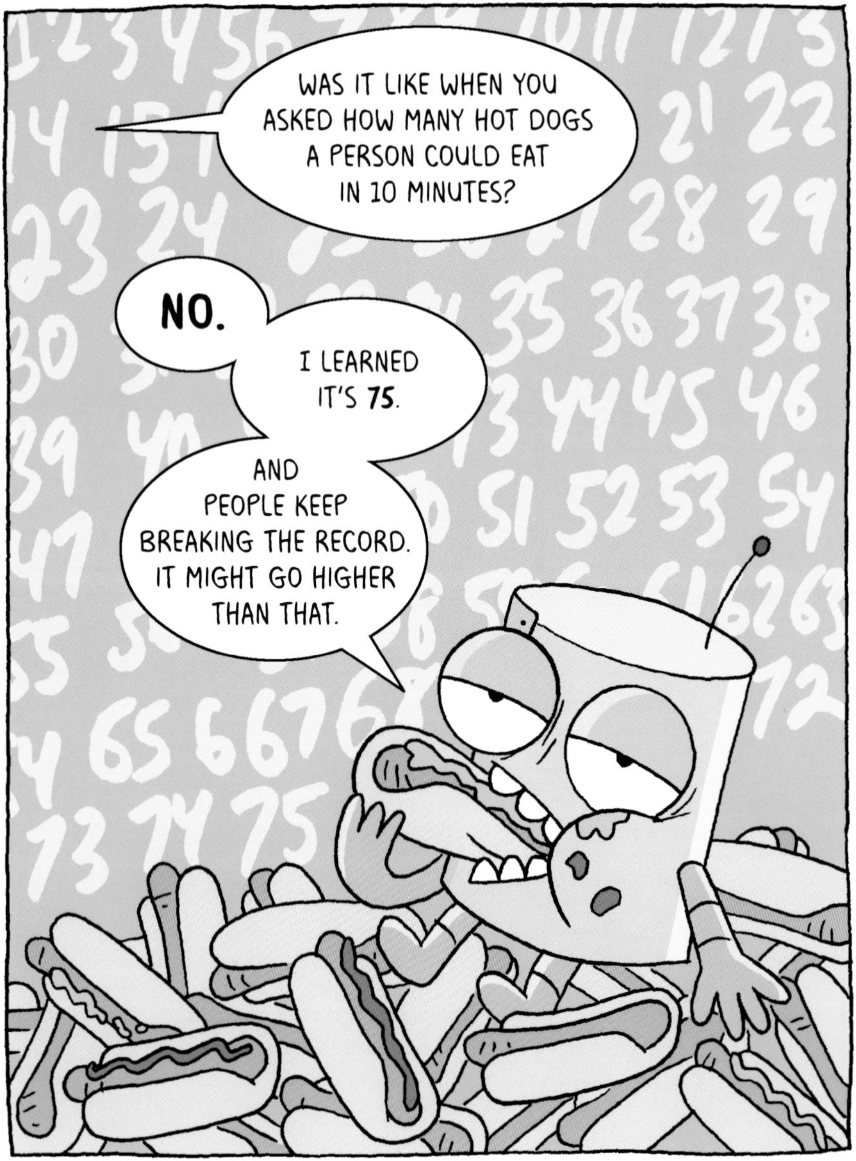
WAS IT LIKE WHEN YOU ASKED HOW MANY HOT DOGS A PERSON COULD EAT IN 10 MINUTES?
NO.
I LEARNED IT'S 75.
AND PEOPLE KEEP BREAKING THE RECORD. IT MIGHT GO HIGHER THAN THAT.

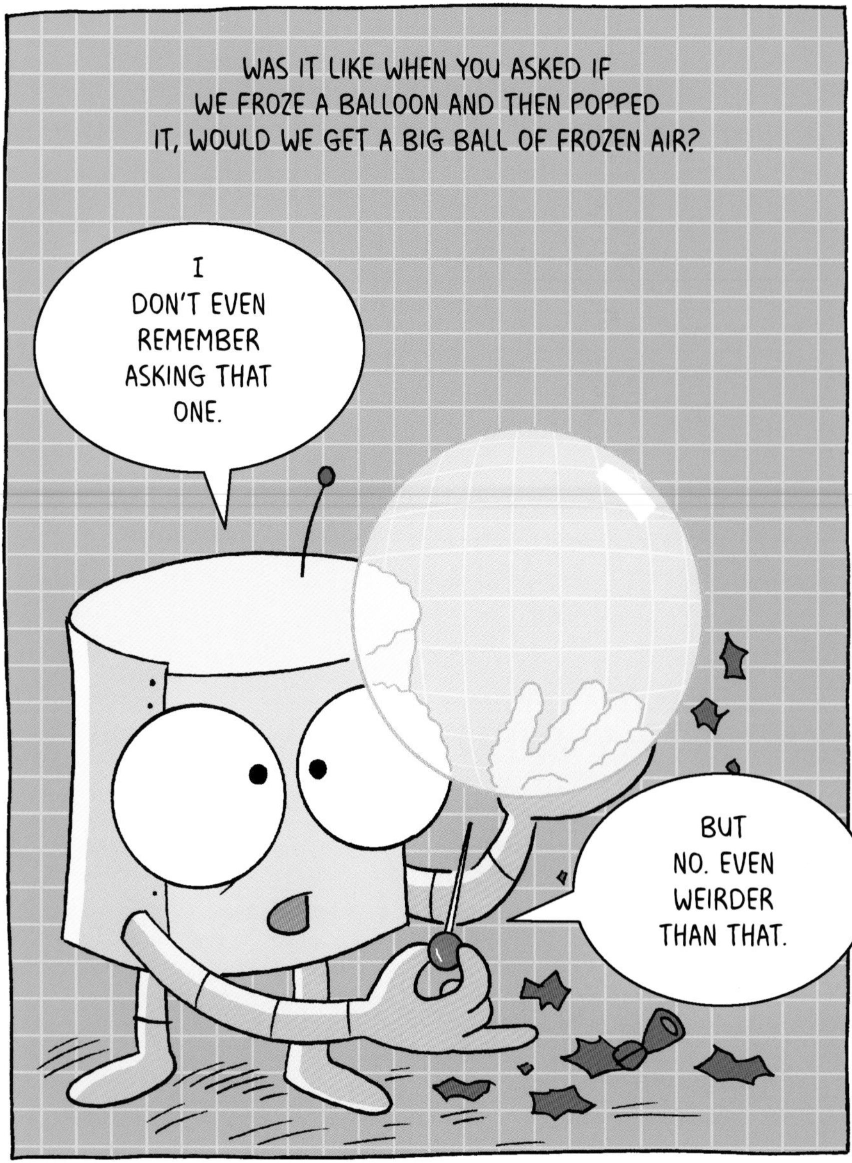
WAS IT LIKE WHEN YOU ASKED IF WE FROZE A BALLOON AND THEN POPPED IT, WOULD WE GET A BIG BALL OF FROZEN AIR?
I DON'T EVEN REMEMBER ASKING THAT ONE.
BUT NO. EVEN WEIRDER THAN THAT.

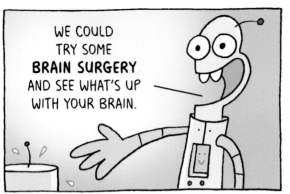

WE COULD TRY SOME **BRAIN SURGERY** AND SEE WHAT'S UP WITH YOUR BRAIN.

I'VE ALWAYS THOUGHT THAT SOUNDED FUN.

POP!

OKAY, SO I OPENED YOUR HEAD. I CAN SEE YOUR **BRAIN**.

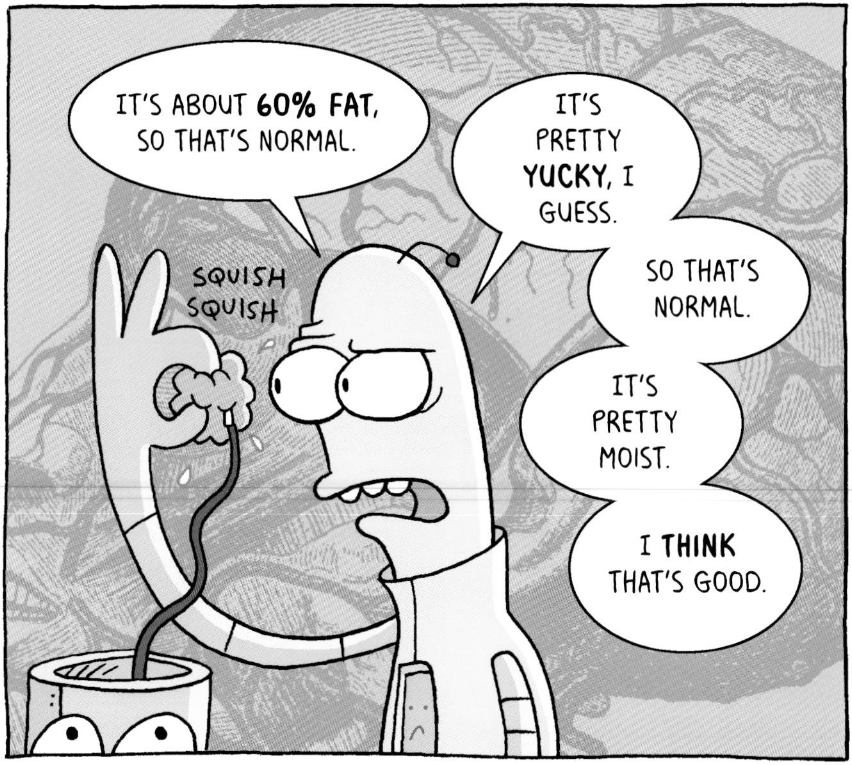
IT'S ABOUT **60% FAT**, SO THAT'S NORMAL.
IT'S PRETTY **YUCKY**, I GUESS.
SO THAT'S NORMAL.
IT'S PRETTY MOIST.
I **THINK** THAT'S GOOD.
SQUISH SQUISH

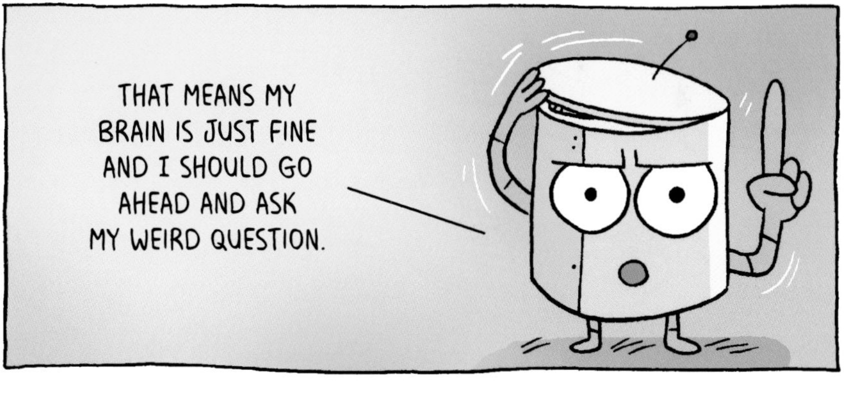
THAT MEANS MY BRAIN IS JUST FINE AND I SHOULD GO AHEAD AND ASK MY WEIRD QUESTION.

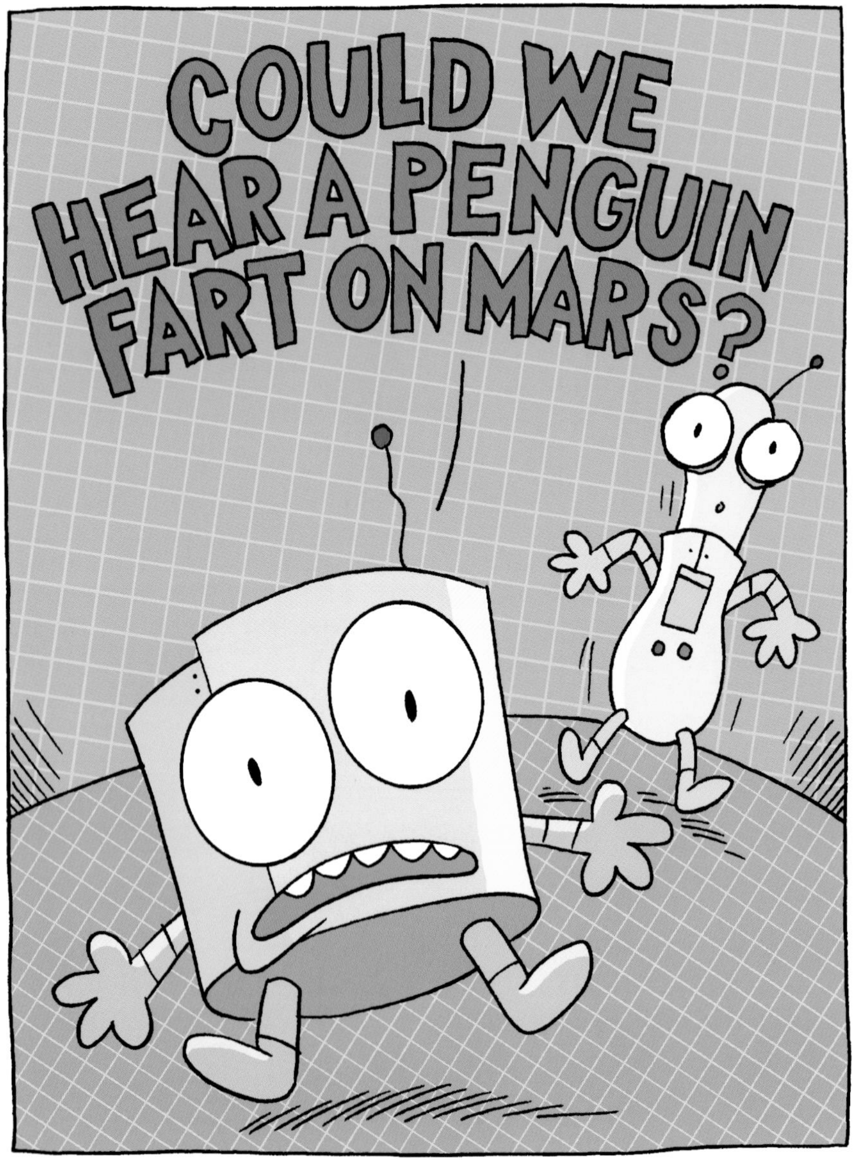
COULD WE HEAR A PENGUIN FART ON MARS?

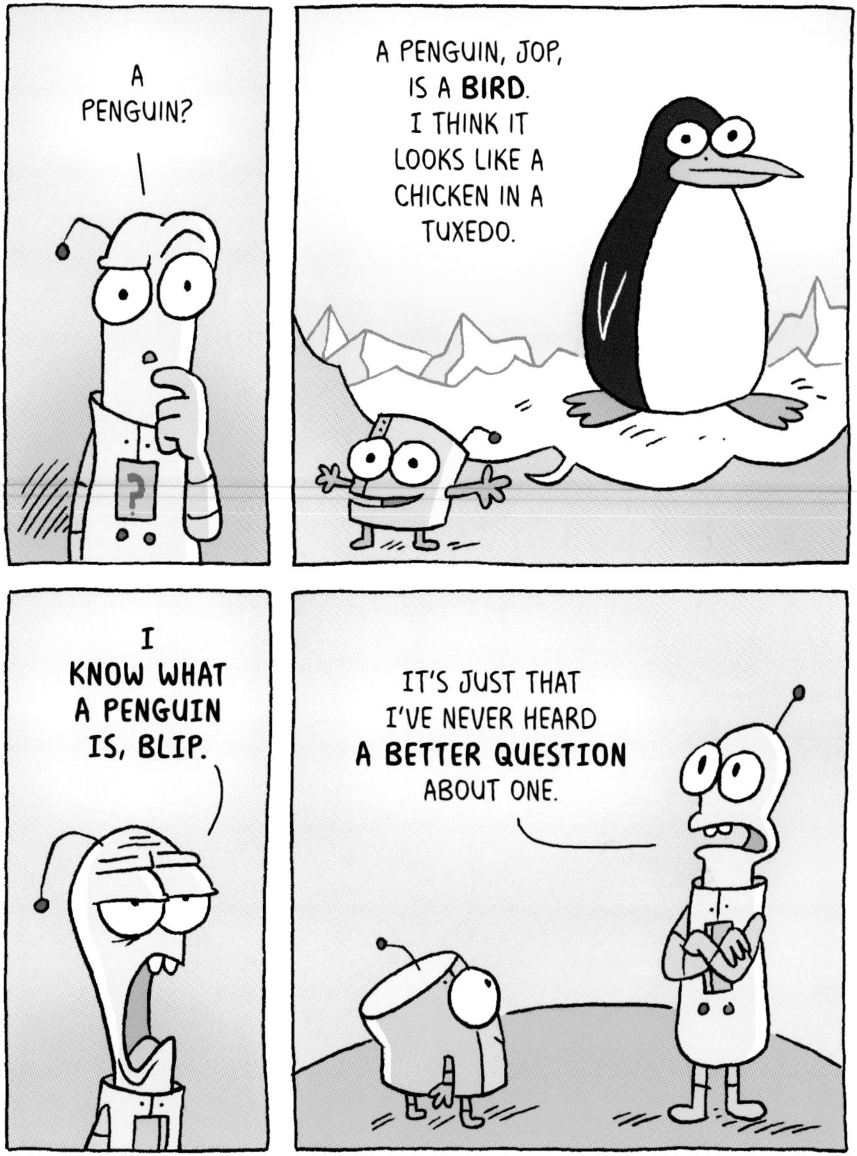
A PENGUIN?
A PENGUIN, JOP, IS A **BIRD**. I THINK IT LOOKS LIKE A CHICKEN IN A TUXEDO.
I KNOW WHAT A PENGUIN IS, BLIP.
IT'S JUST THAT I'VE NEVER HEARD **A BETTER QUESTION** ABOUT ONE.

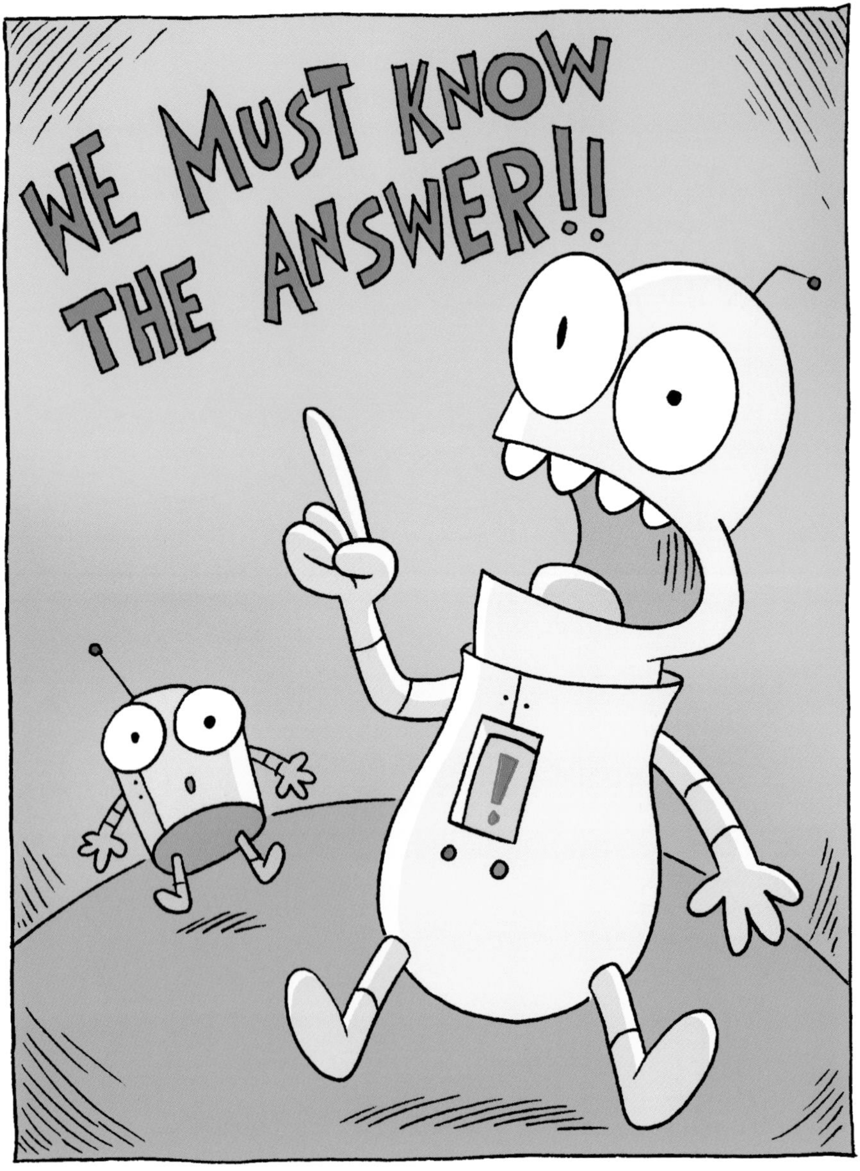
WE MUST KNOW THE ANSWER!!

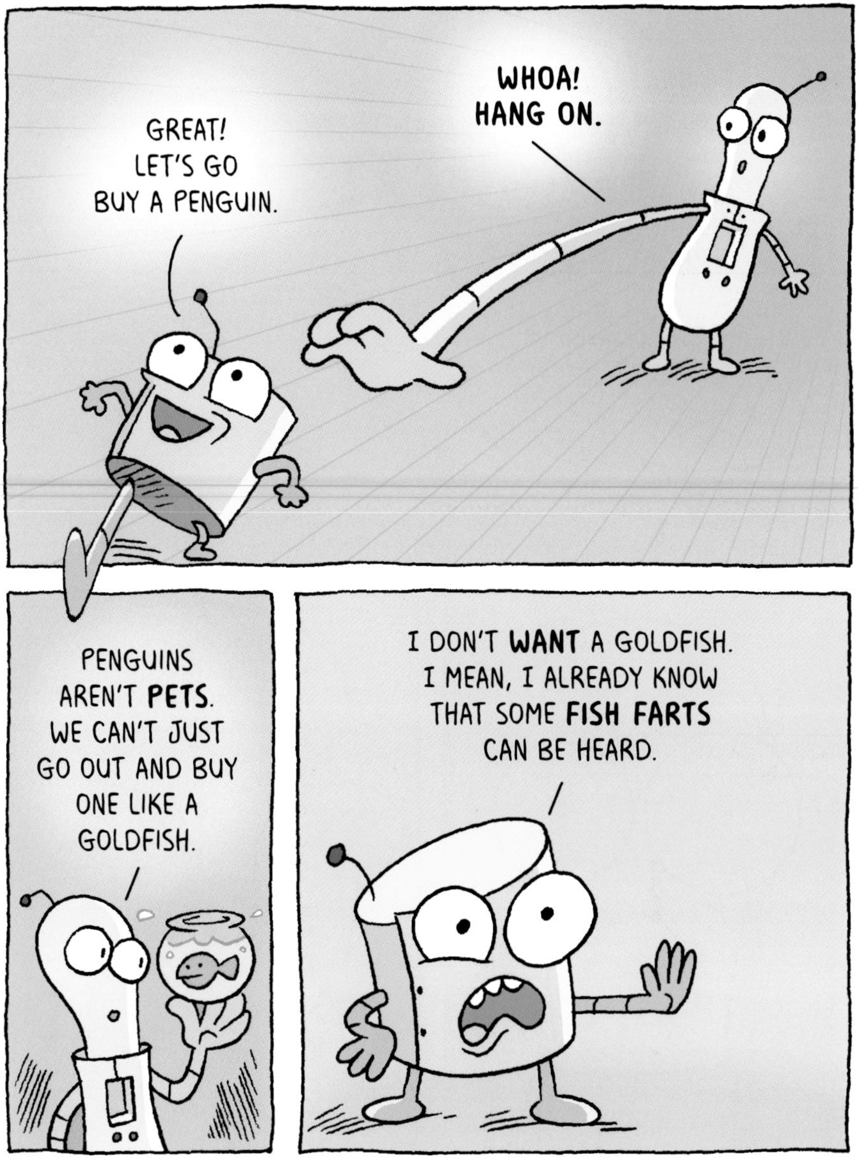
GREAT! LET'S GO BUY A PENGUIN.
WHOA! HANG ON.
PENGUINS AREN'T **PETS**. WE CAN'T JUST GO OUT AND BUY ONE LIKE A GOLDFISH.
I DON'T **WANT** A GOLDFISH. I MEAN, I ALREADY KNOW THAT SOME **FISH FARTS** CAN BE HEARD.

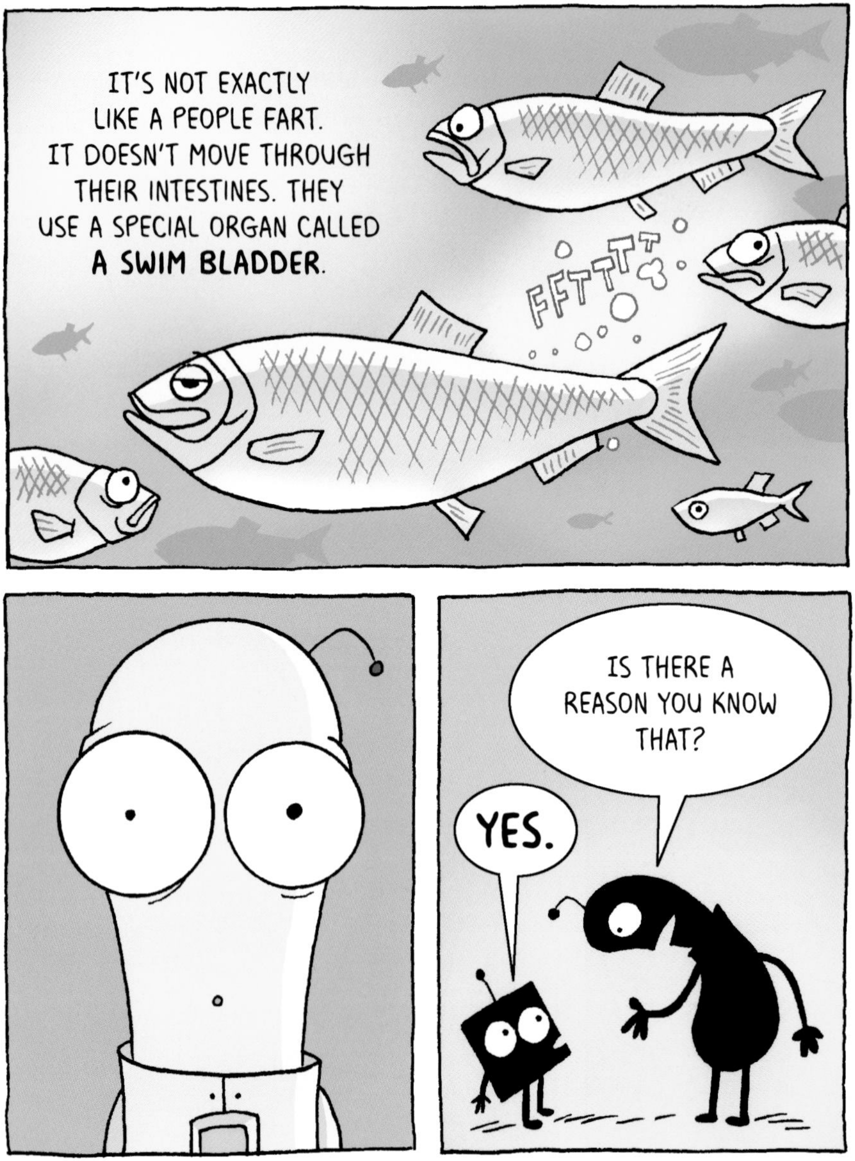
IT'S NOT EXACTLY LIKE A PEOPLE FART. IT DOESN'T MOVE THROUGH THEIR INTESTINES. THEY USE A SPECIAL ORGAN CALLED **A SWIM BLADDER**.
FFTTTTT
IS THERE A REASON YOU KNOW THAT?
YES.

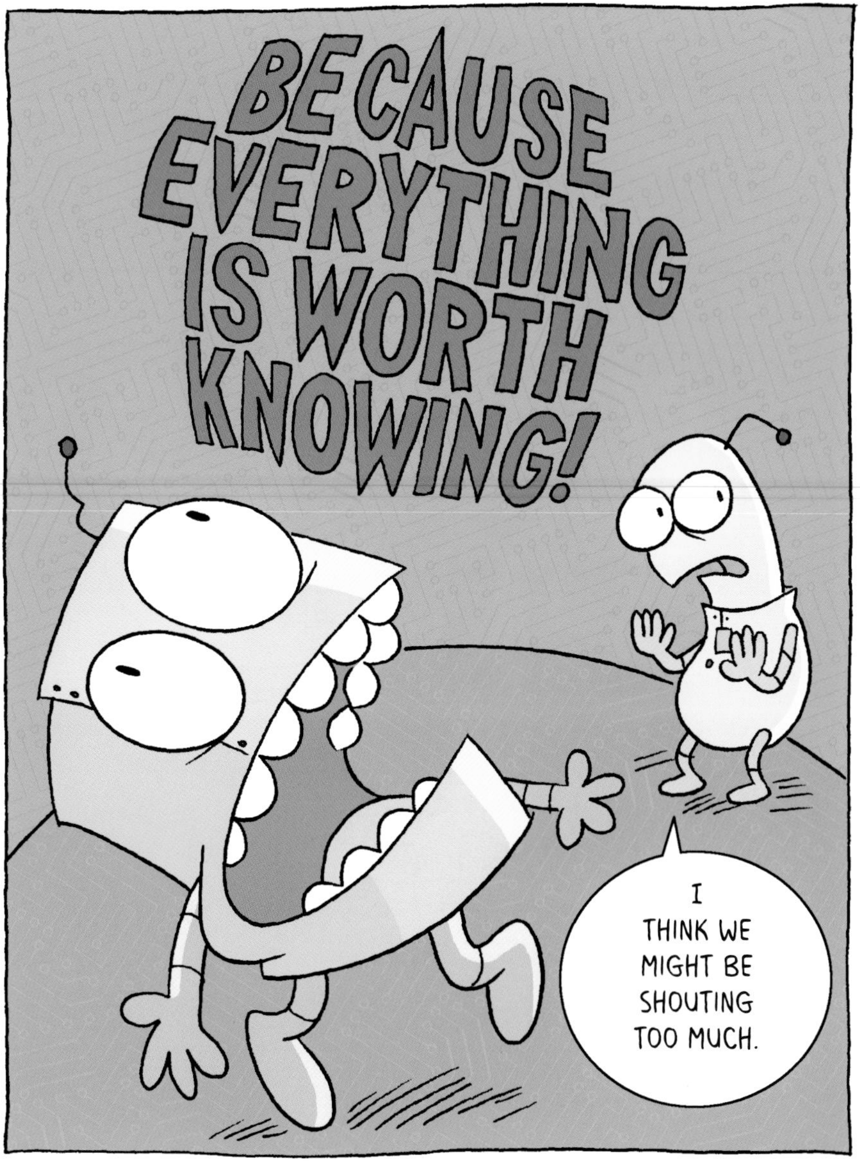
BECAUSE EVERYTHING IS WORTH KNOWING!
I THINK WE MIGHT BE SHOUTING TOO MUCH.

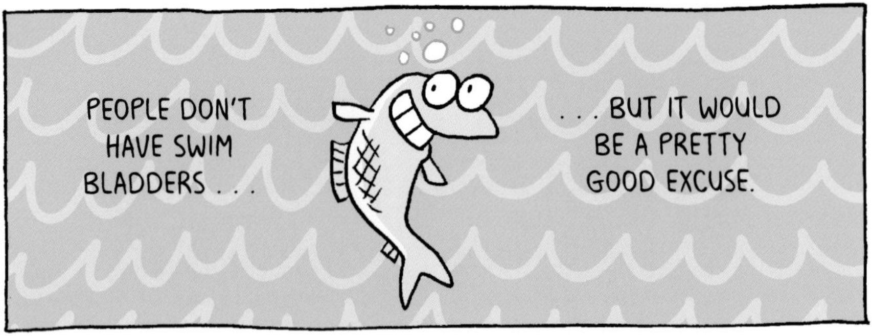
PEOPLE DON'T HAVE SWIM BLADDERS . . .
. . . BUT IT WOULD BE A PRETTY GOOD EXCUSE.

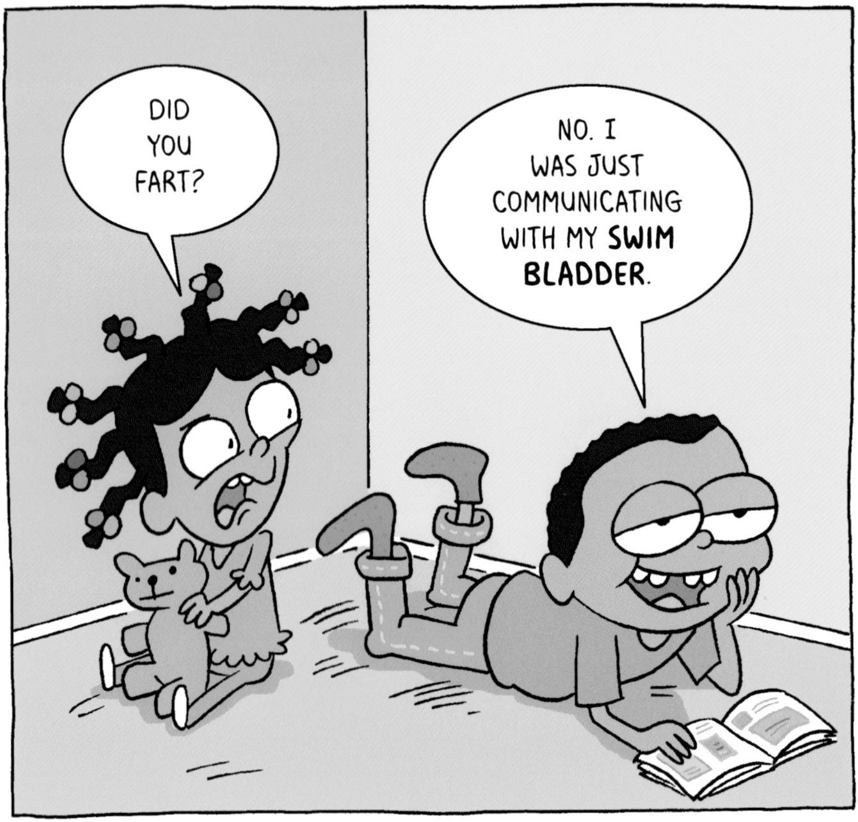
DID YOU FART?
NO. I WAS JUST COMMUNICATING WITH MY **SWIM BLADDER**.

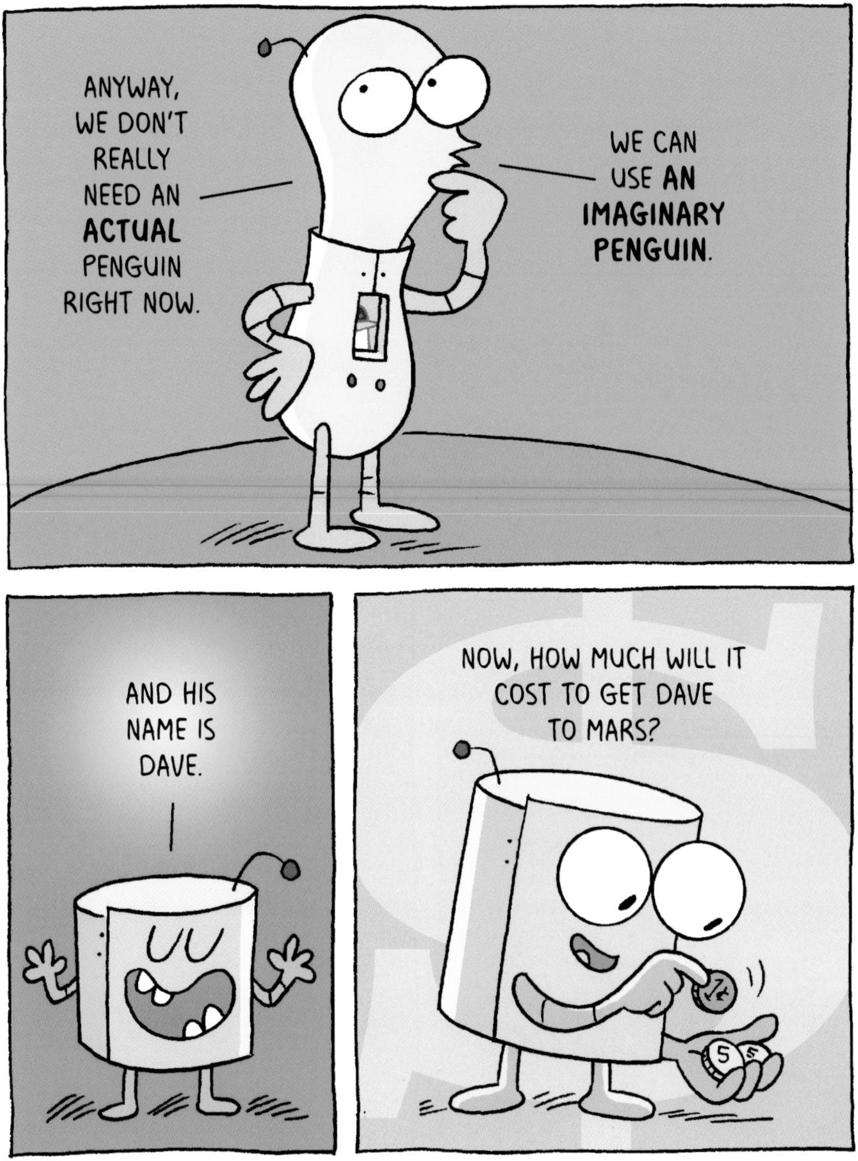
ANYWAY, WE DON'T REALLY NEED AN **ACTUAL** PENGUIN RIGHT NOW.
WE CAN USE **AN IMAGINARY PENGUIN**.
AND HIS NAME IS DAVE.
NOW, HOW MUCH WILL IT COST TO GET DAVE TO MARS?

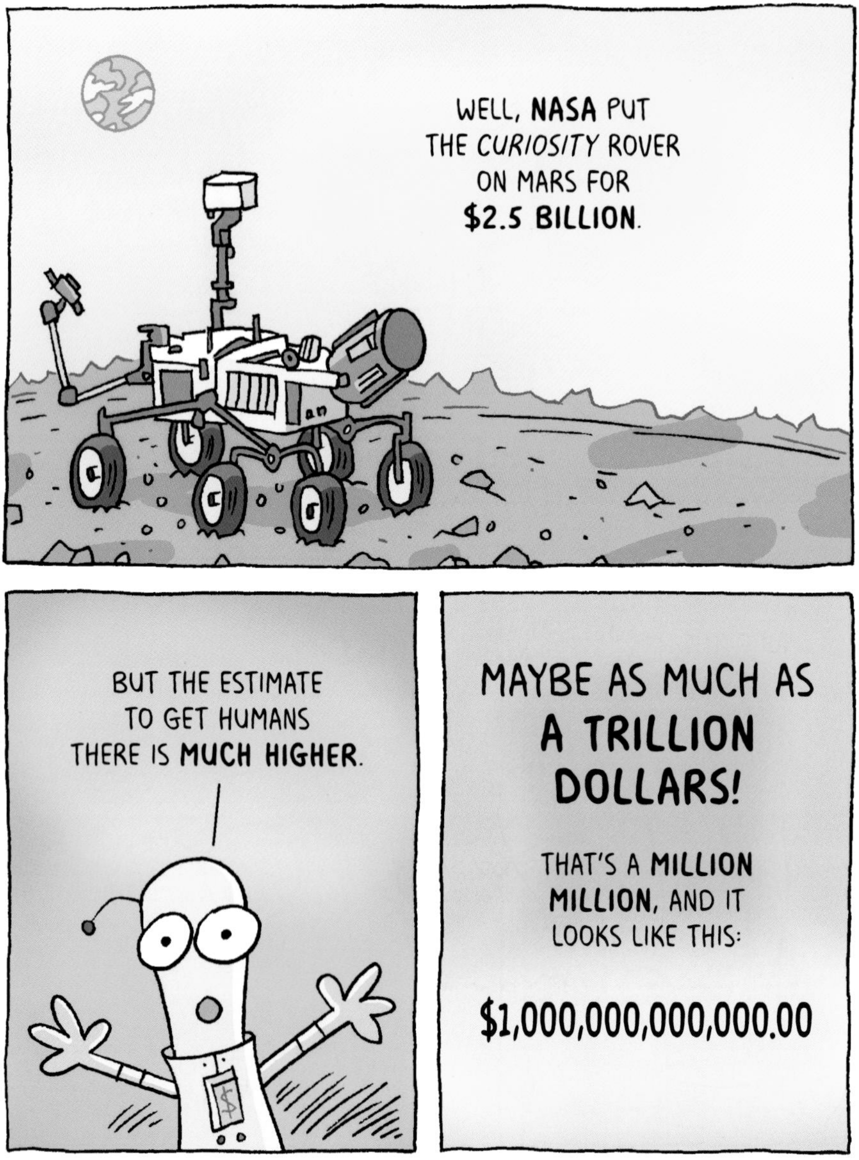
WELL, NASA PUT THE CURIOSITY ROVER ON MARS FOR $2.5 BILLION.
BUT THE ESTIMATE TO GET HUMANS THERE IS MUCH HIGHER.
MAYBE AS MUCH AS A TRILLION DOLLARS!
THAT'S A MILLION MILLION, AND IT LOOKS LIKE THIS:
$1,000,000,000,000.00

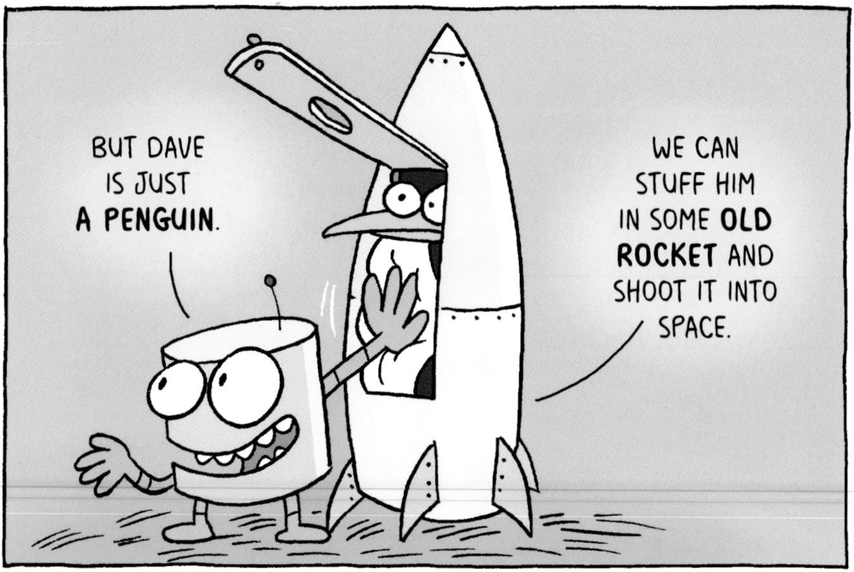
BUT DAVE IS JUST **A PENGUIN**.
WE CAN STUFF HIM IN SOME **OLD ROCKET** AND SHOOT IT INTO SPACE.

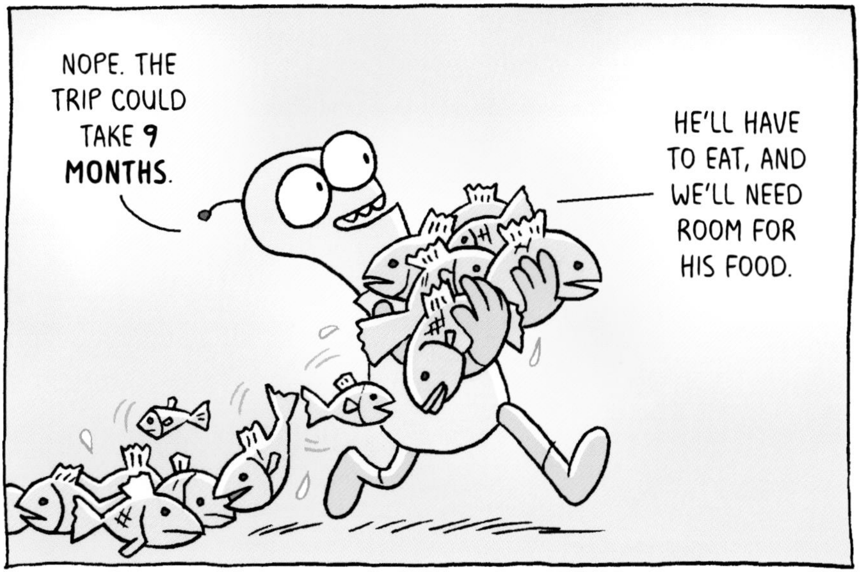
NOPE. THE TRIP COULD TAKE **9 MONTHS**.
HE'LL HAVE TO EAT, AND WE'LL NEED ROOM FOR HIS FOOD.

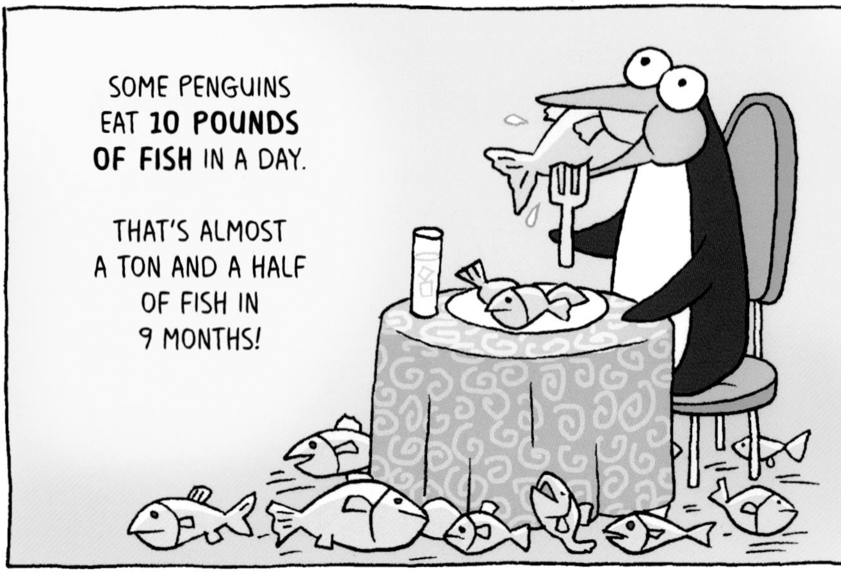
SOME PENGUINS EAT **10 POUNDS OF FISH** IN A DAY.
THAT'S ALMOST A TON AND A HALF OF FISH IN 9 MONTHS!

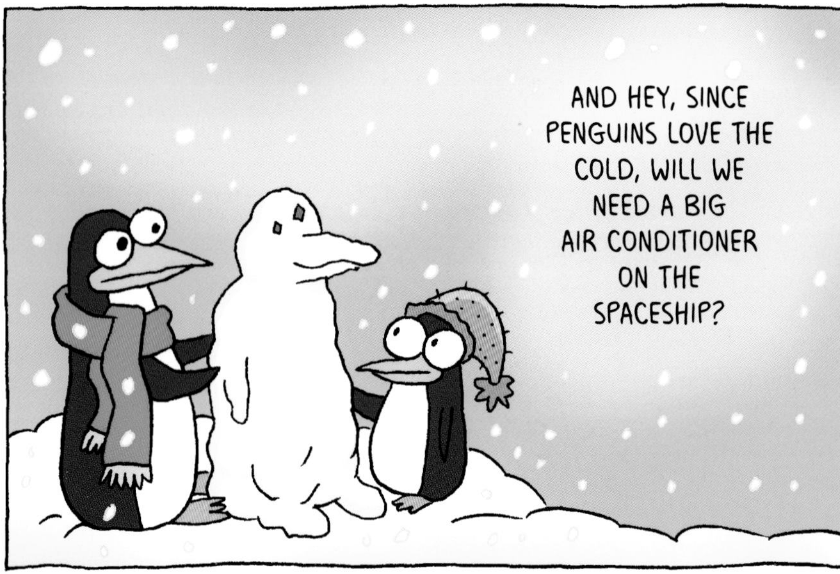
AND HEY, SINCE PENGUINS LOVE THE COLD, WILL WE NEED A BIG AIR CONDITIONER ON THE SPACESHIP?

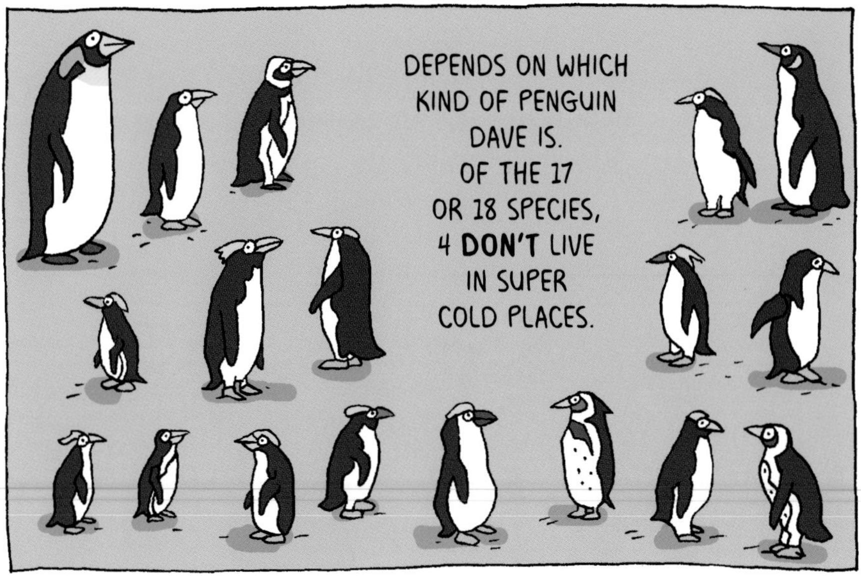
DEPENDS ON WHICH KIND OF PENGUIN DAVE IS. OF THE 17 OR 18 SPECIES, 4 **DON'T** LIVE IN SUPER COLD PLACES.

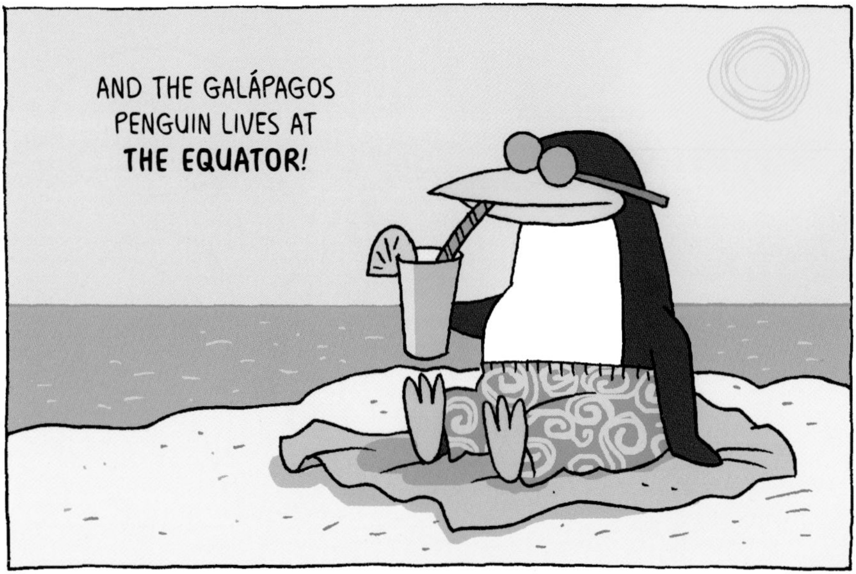
AND THE GALÁPAGOS PENGUIN LIVES AT **THE EQUATOR**!

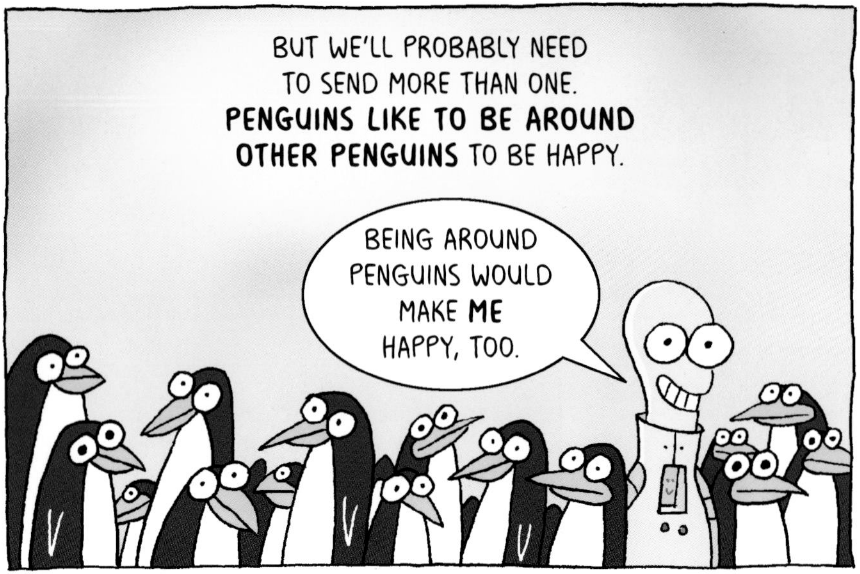
BUT WE'LL PROBABLY NEED TO SEND MORE THAN ONE. **PENGUINS LIKE TO BE AROUND OTHER PENGUINS** TO BE HAPPY.
BEING AROUND PENGUINS WOULD MAKE **ME** HAPPY, TOO.

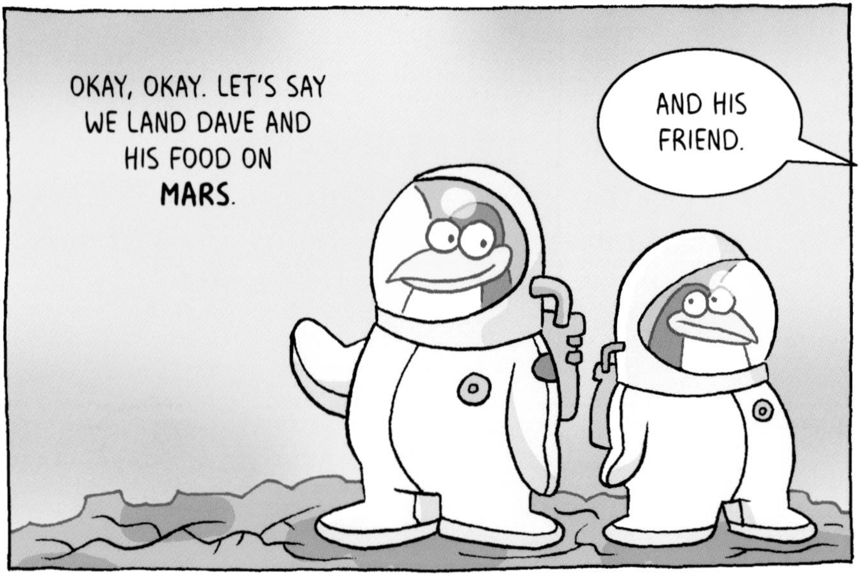
OKAY, OKAY. LET'S SAY WE LAND DAVE AND HIS FOOD ON **MARS**.
AND HIS FRIEND.

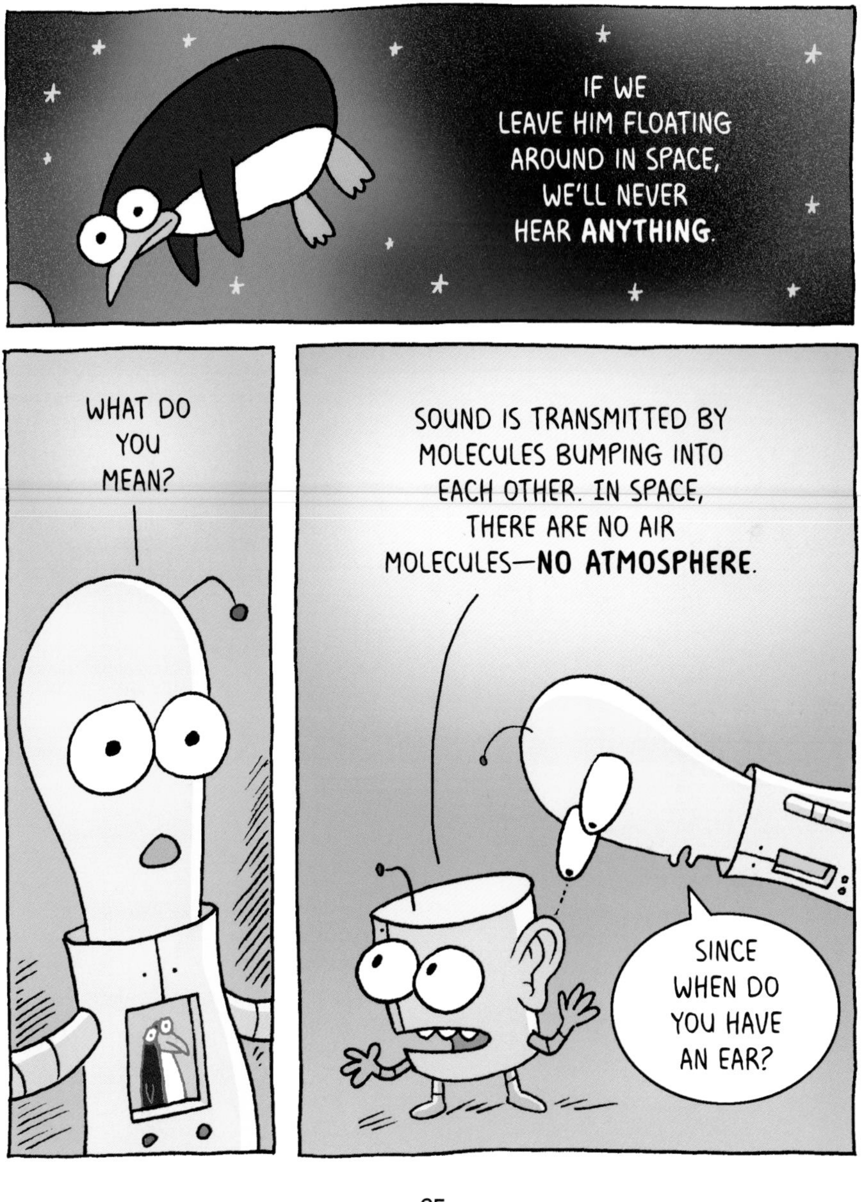
IF WE LEAVE HIM FLOATING AROUND IN SPACE, WE'LL NEVER HEAR **ANYTHING**.
WHAT DO YOU MEAN?
SOUND IS TRANSMITTED BY MOLECULES BUMPING INTO EACH OTHER. IN SPACE, THERE ARE NO AIR MOLECULES—**NO ATMOSPHERE**.
SINCE WHEN DO YOU HAVE AN EAR?

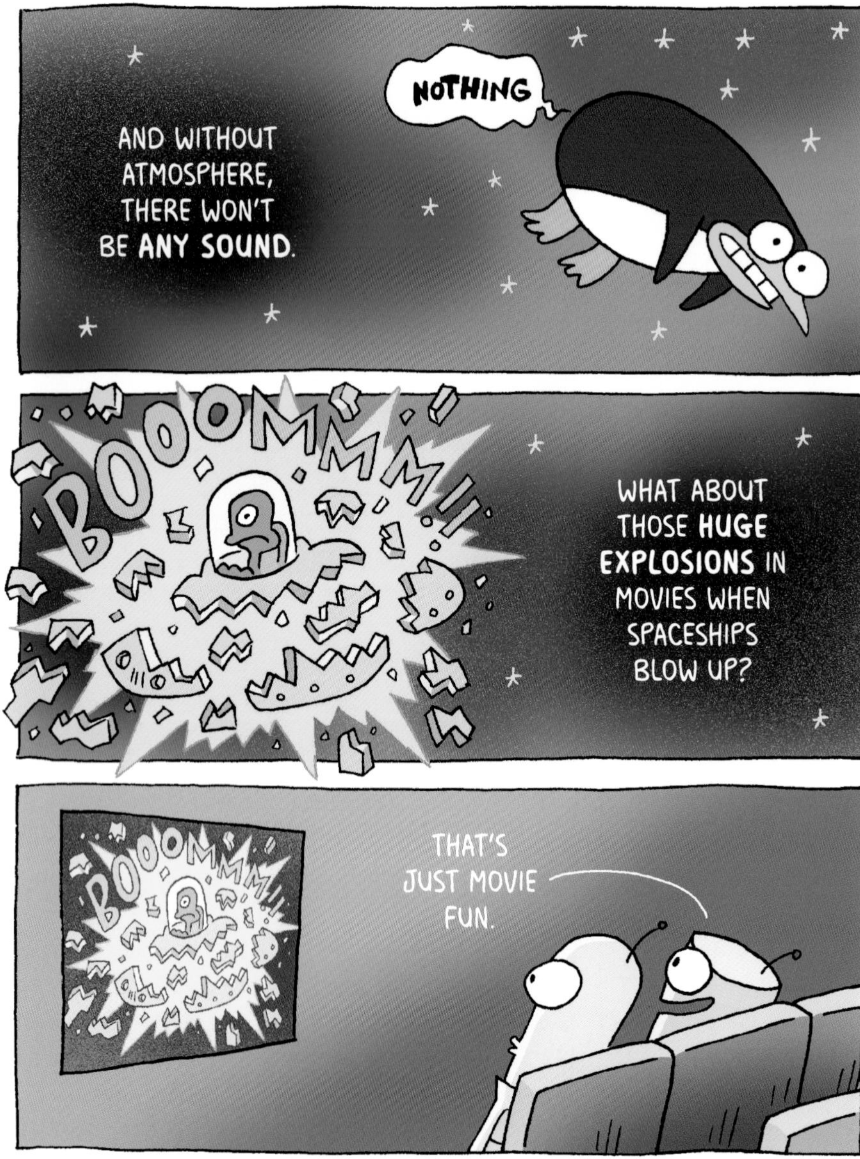
AND WITHOUT ATMOSPHERE, THERE WON'T BE **ANY SOUND**.
NOTHING
BOOOMMM!!
WHAT ABOUT THOSE **HUGE EXPLOSIONS** IN MOVIES WHEN SPACESHIPS BLOW UP?
BOOOMMM!!
THAT'S JUST MOVIE FUN.

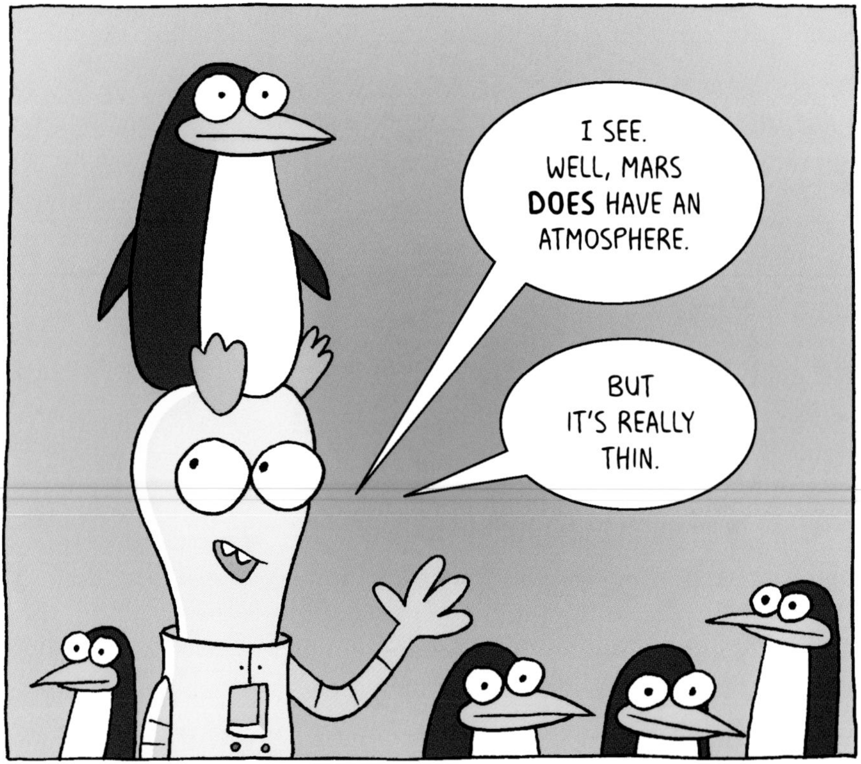
I SEE.
WELL, MARS **DOES** HAVE AN ATMOSPHERE.
BUT IT'S REALLY THIN.

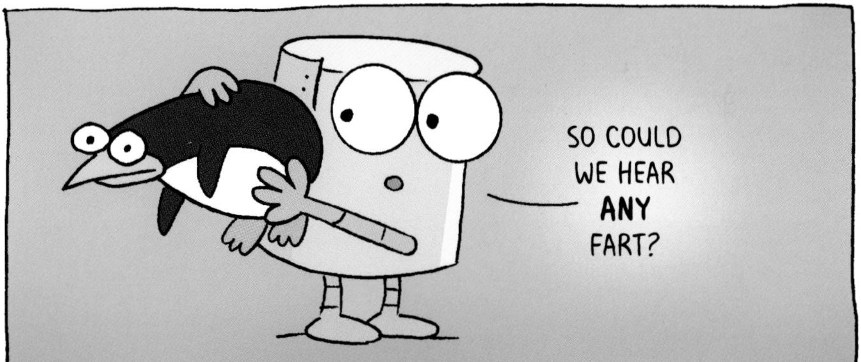
SO COULD WE HEAR **ANY** FART?

MAYBE. BUT I THINK IT WOULD NEED TO BE **LOUD**.

MY GRANDMA'S FARTS ARE **PRETTY LOUD**.

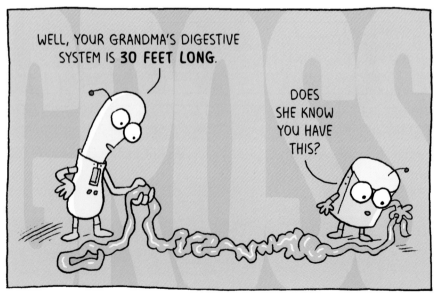

WELL, YOUR GRANDMA'S DIGESTIVE SYSTEM IS **30 FEET LONG**.

DOES SHE KNOW YOU HAVE THIS?

UM. YEAH.

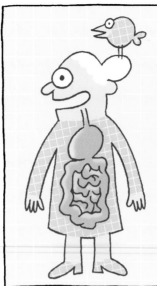

IN A **LONG** DIGESTIVE SYSTEM, THERE'S A LOT OF TIME FOR THE FOOD GRANDMA EATS TO MAKE **GAS**, AND THAT GAS **BUILDS UP**.

BIRDS HAVE **SHORT** DIGESTIVE SYSTEMS.

AND THEY POOP **REALLY OFTEN**. SO GAS NEVER BUILDS UP.

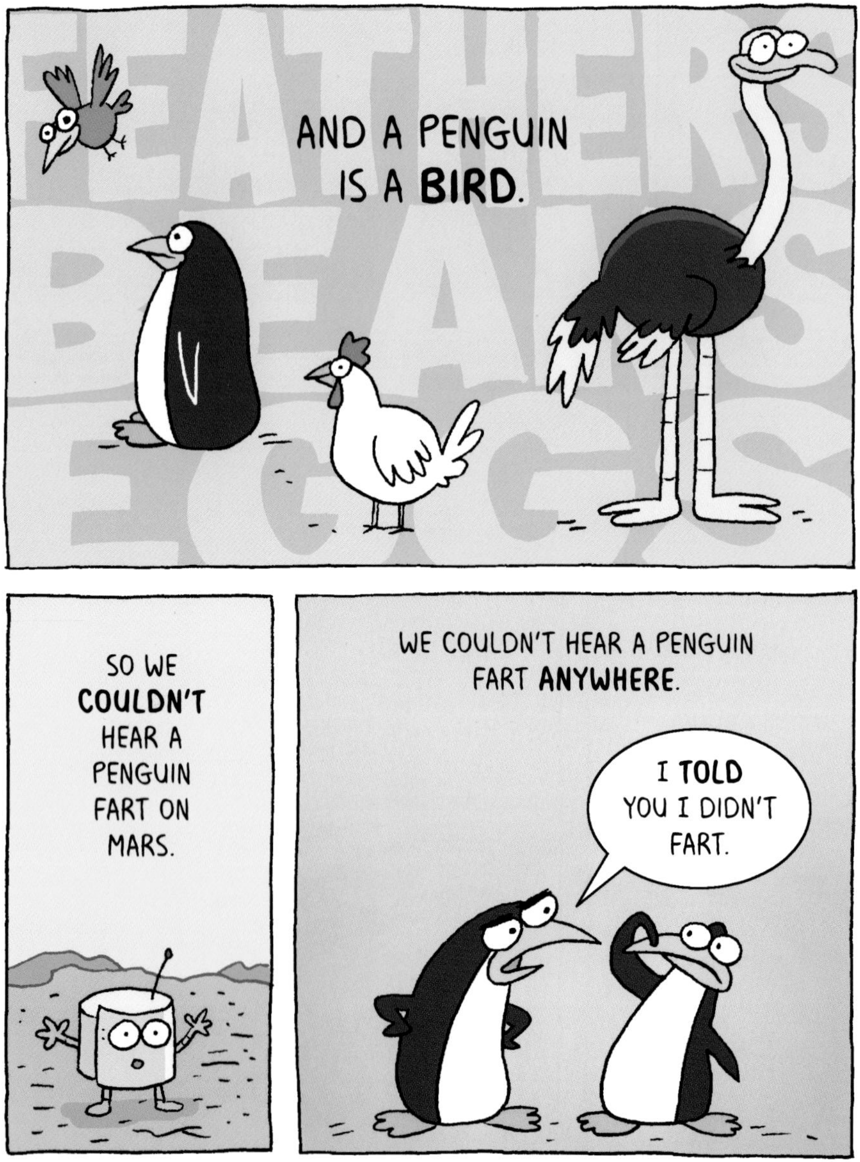
AND A PENGUIN IS A **BIRD**.
SO WE **COULDN'T** HEAR A PENGUIN FART ON MARS.
WE COULDN'T HEAR A PENGUIN FART **ANYWHERE**.
I **TOLD** YOU I DIDN'T FART.

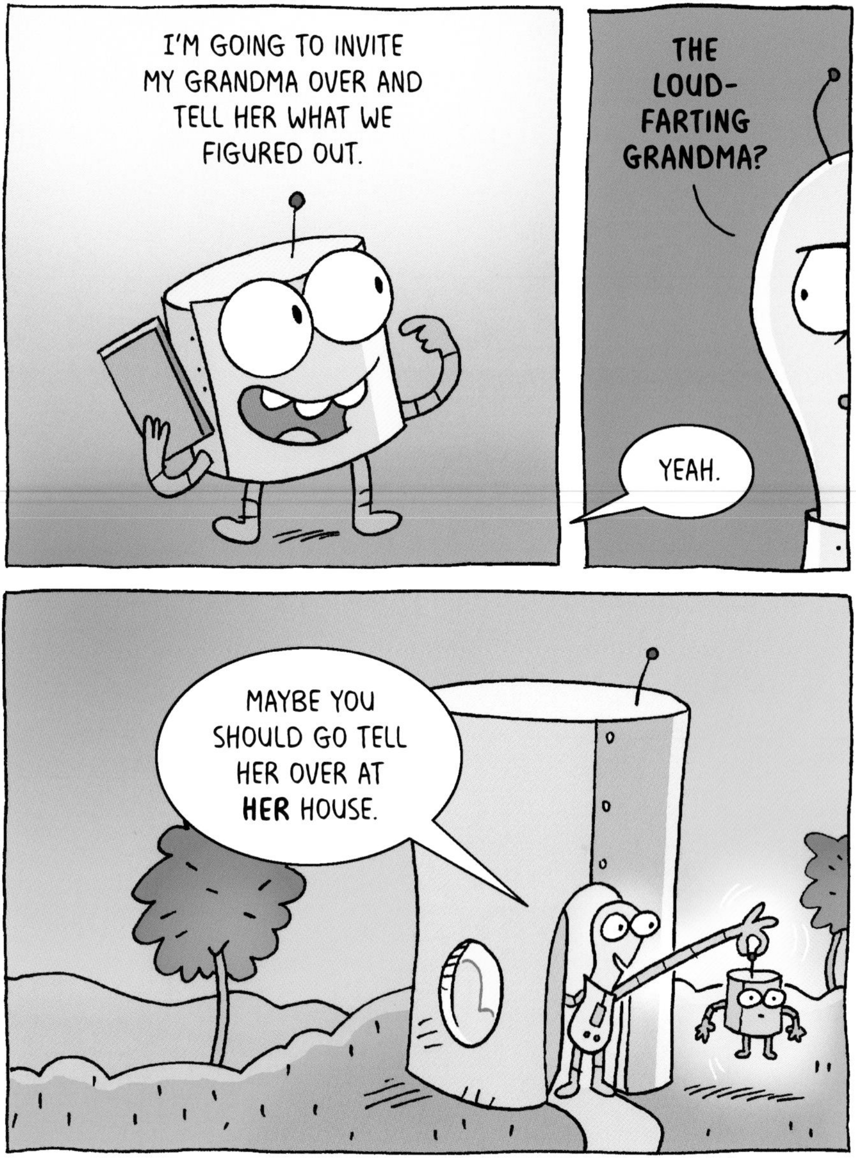
I'M GOING TO INVITE MY GRANDMA OVER AND TELL HER WHAT WE FIGURED OUT.
THE LOUD-FARTING GRANDMA?
YEAH.
MAYBE YOU SHOULD GO TELL HER OVER AT **HER** HOUSE.

CAN YOU FIND THE TWO JOPS THAT ARE **EXACTLY THE SAME?**

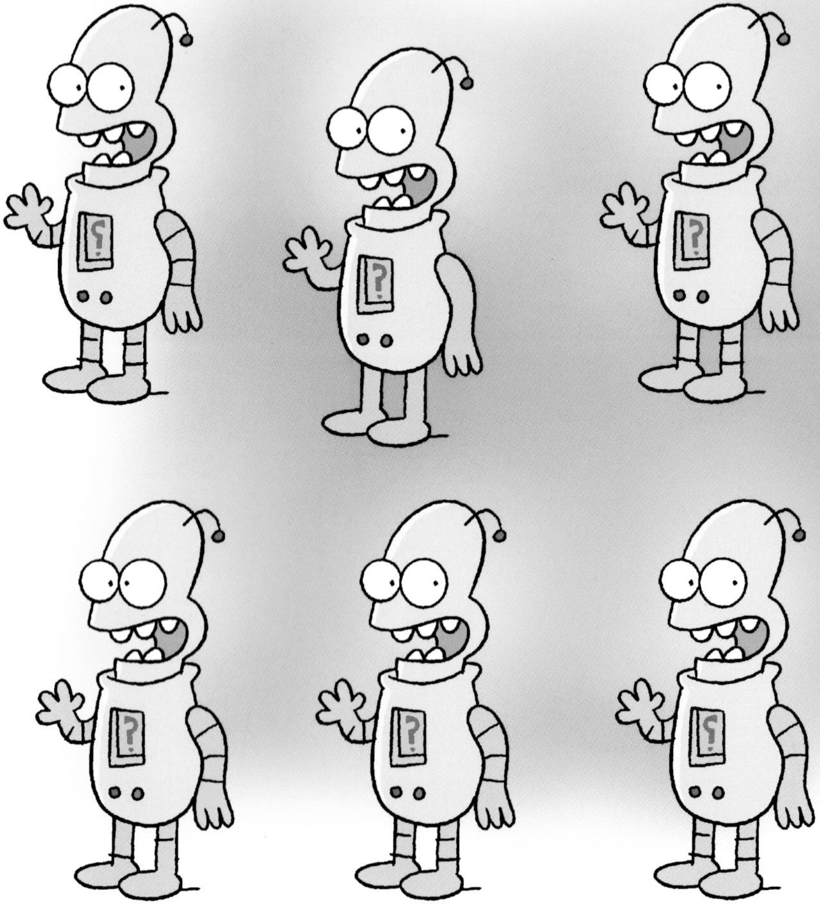

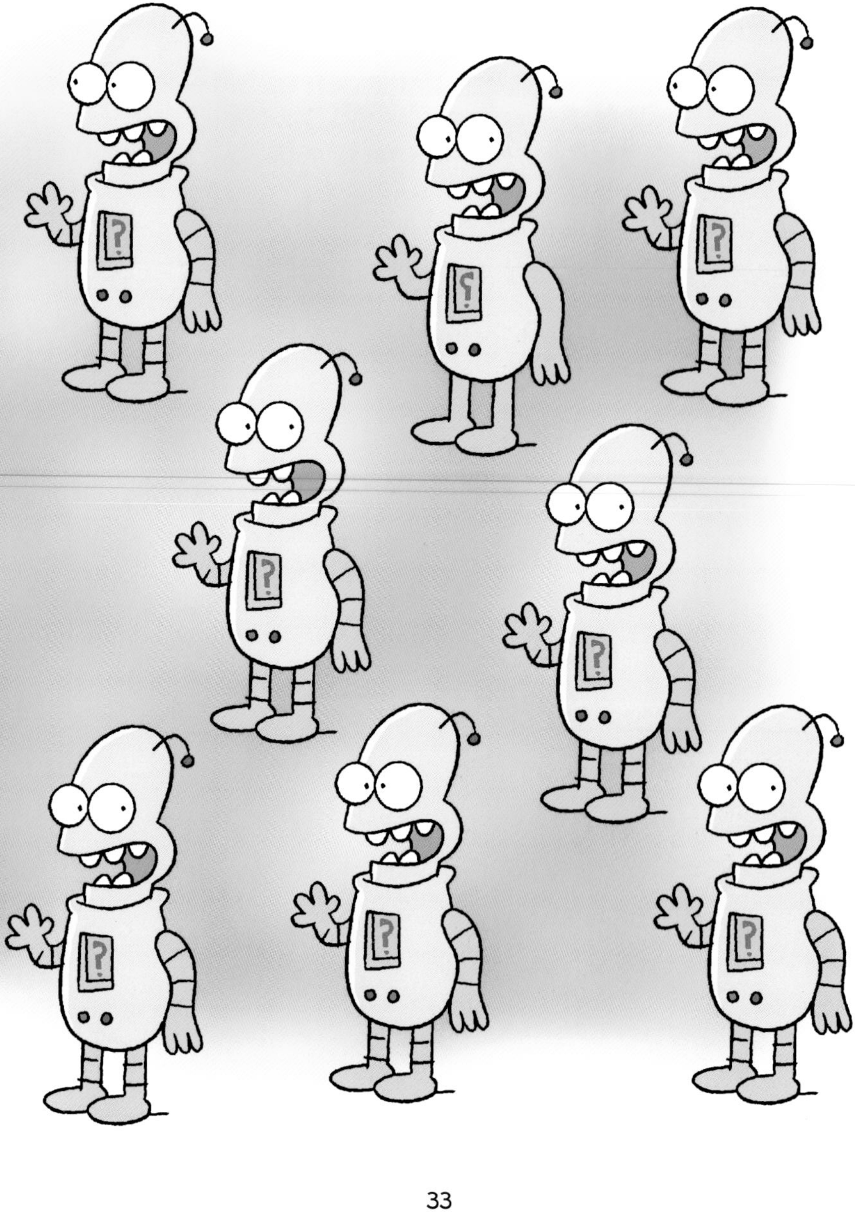

THE DRAGON DILEMMA

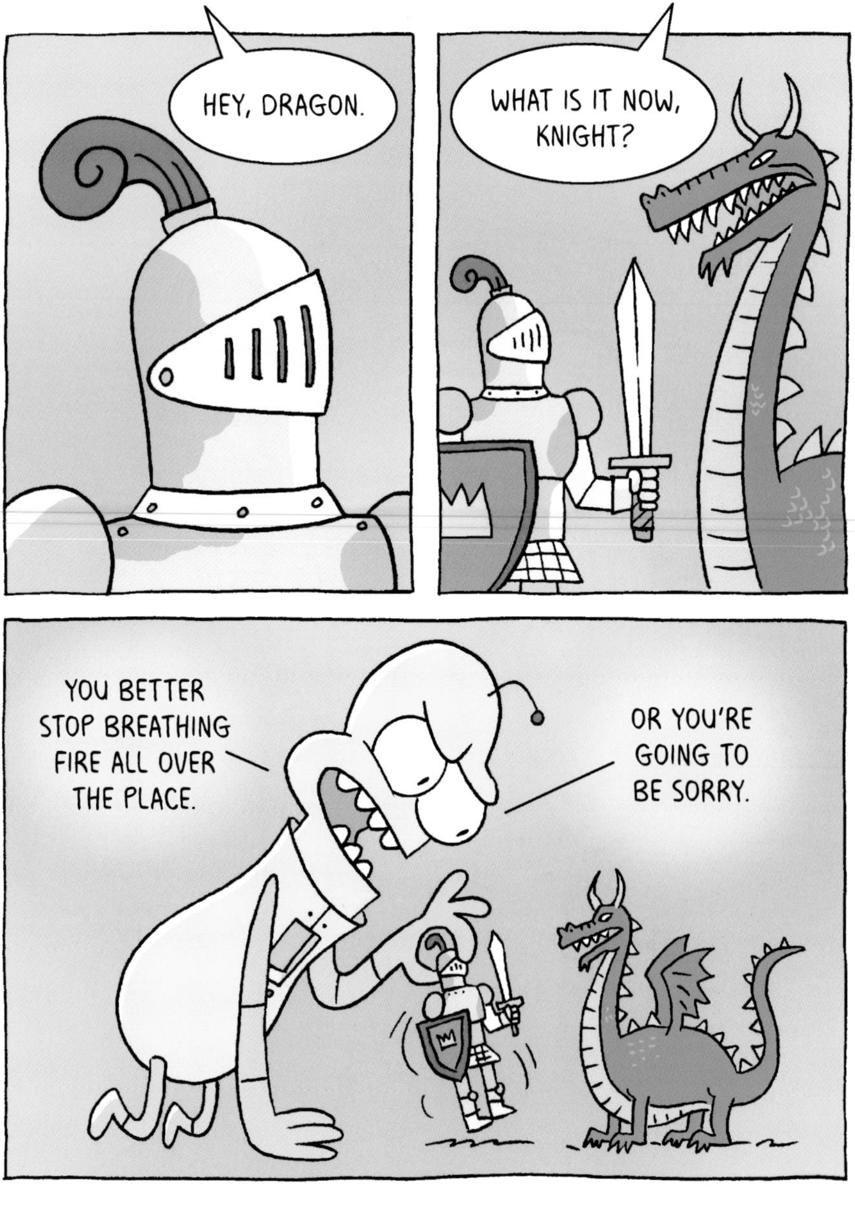
HEY, DRAGON.
WHAT IS IT NOW, KNIGHT?
YOU BETTER STOP BREATHING FIRE ALL OVER THE PLACE.
OR YOU'RE GOING TO BE SORRY.

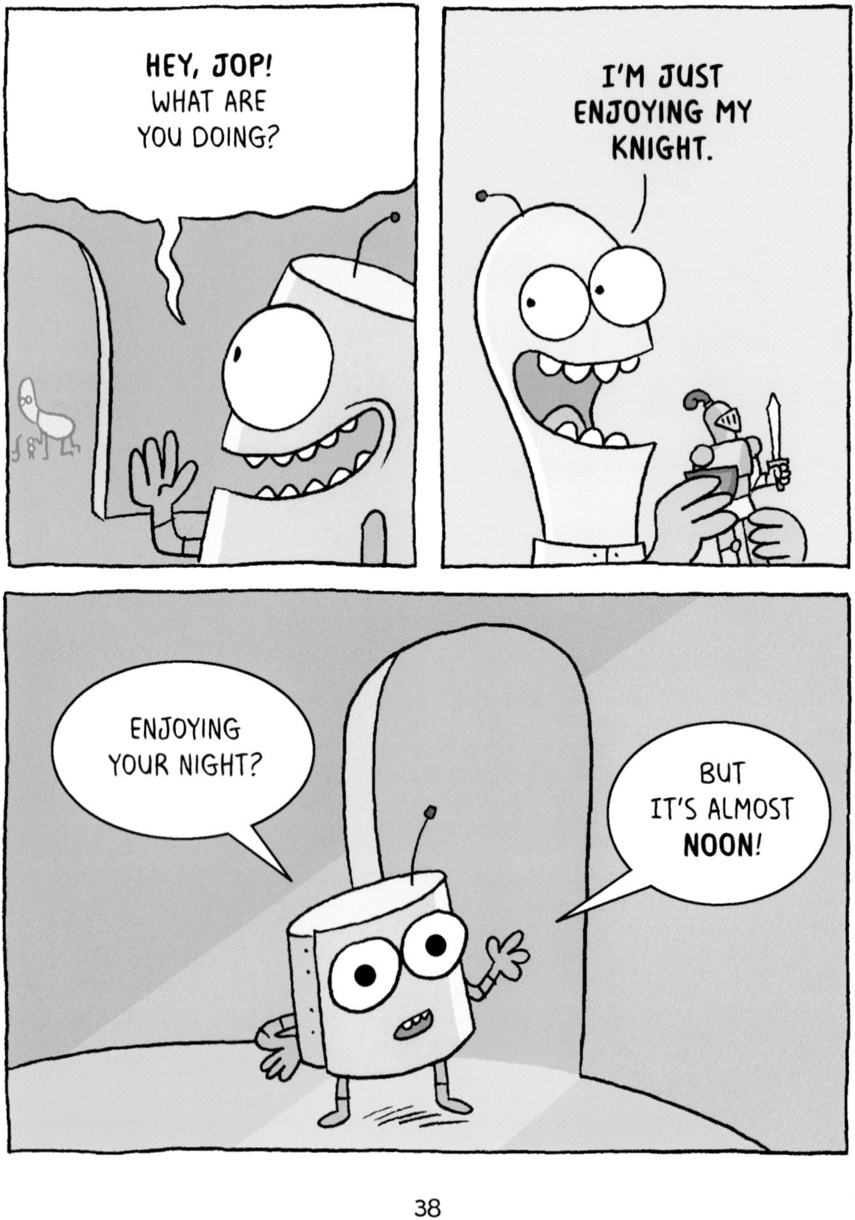
HEY, JOP!
WHAT ARE YOU DOING?
I'M JUST ENJOYING MY KNIGHT.
ENJOYING YOUR NIGHT?
BUT IT'S ALMOST NOON!

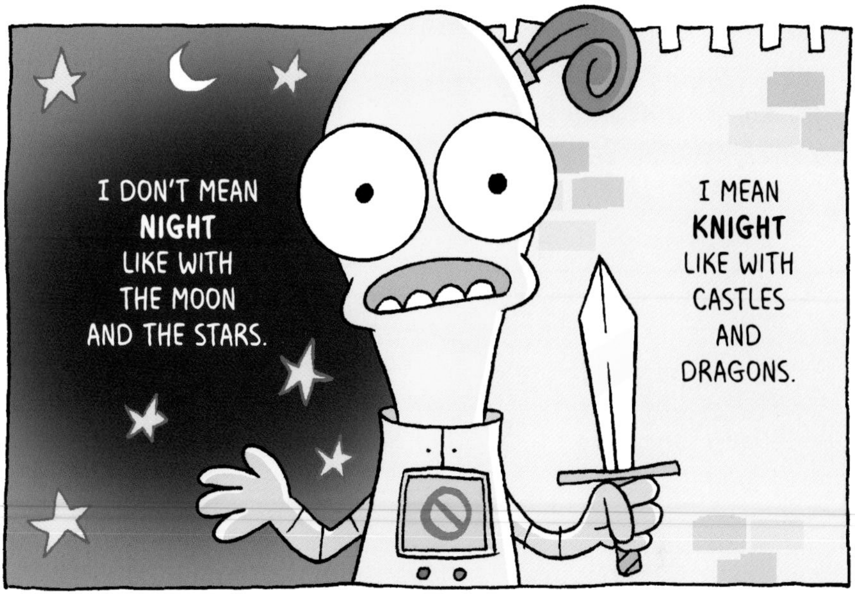
I DON'T MEAN **NIGHT** LIKE WITH THE MOON AND THE STARS.
I MEAN **KNIGHT** LIKE WITH CASTLES AND DRAGONS.

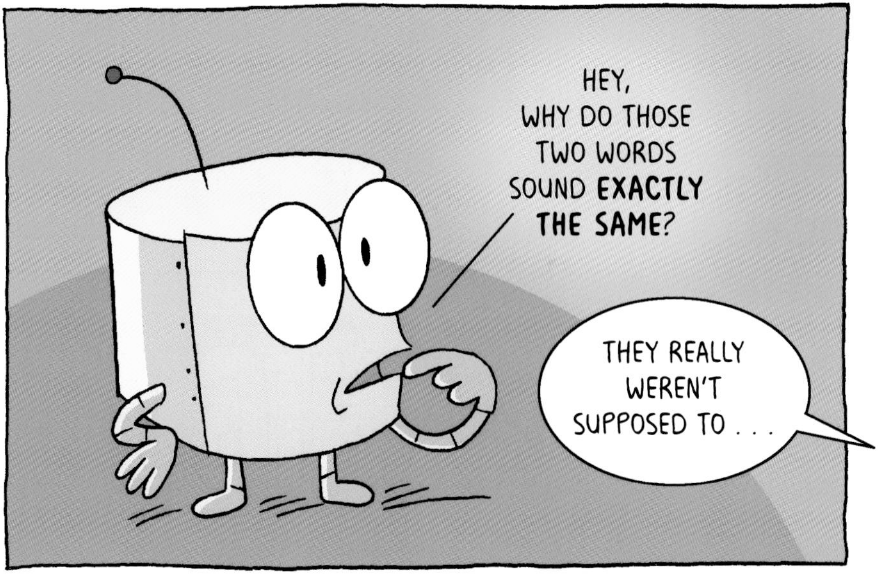
HEY, WHY DO THOSE TWO WORDS SOUND **EXACTLY THE SAME**?
THEY REALLY WEREN'T SUPPOSED TO . . .

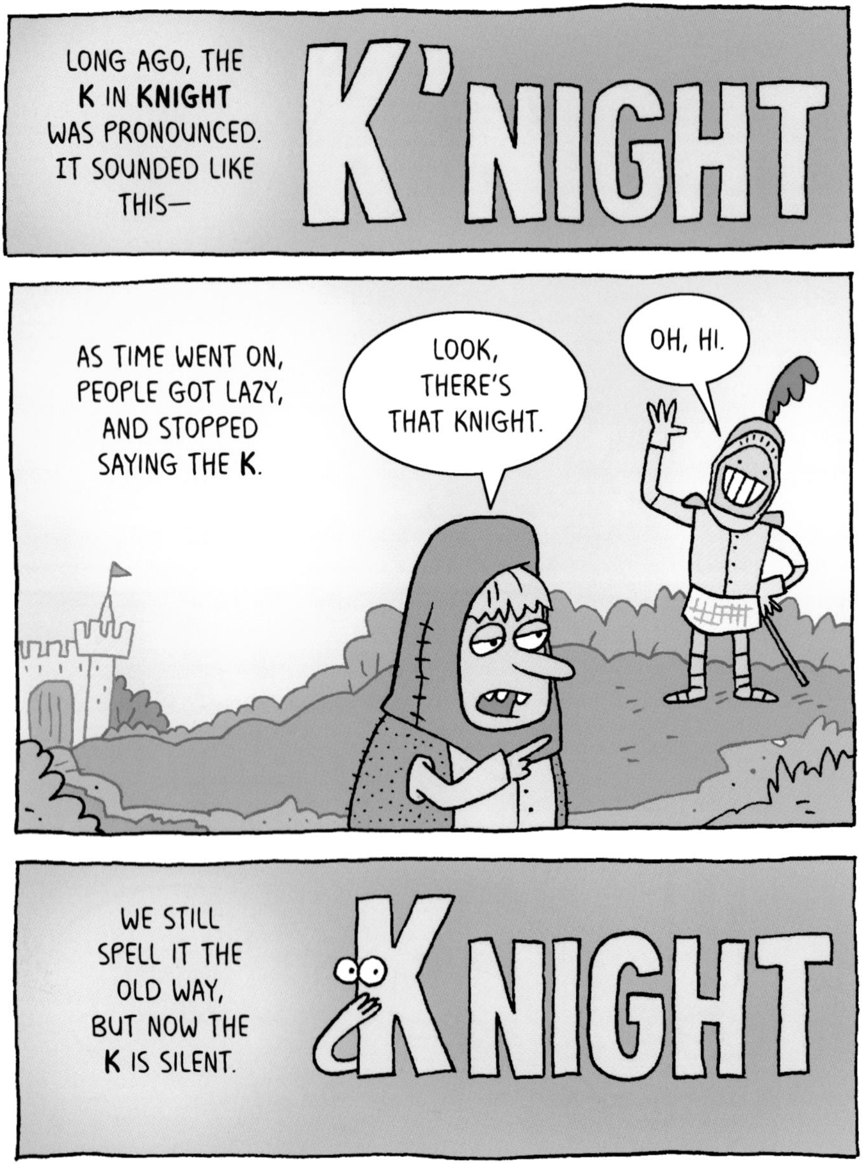
LONG AGO, THE K IN KNIGHT WAS PRONOUNCED. IT SOUNDED LIKE THIS—
K'NIGHT
AS TIME WENT ON, PEOPLE GOT LAZY, AND STOPPED SAYING THE K.
LOOK, THERE'S THAT KNIGHT.
OH, HI.
WE STILL SPELL IT THE OLD WAY, BUT NOW THE K IS SILENT.
KNIGHT

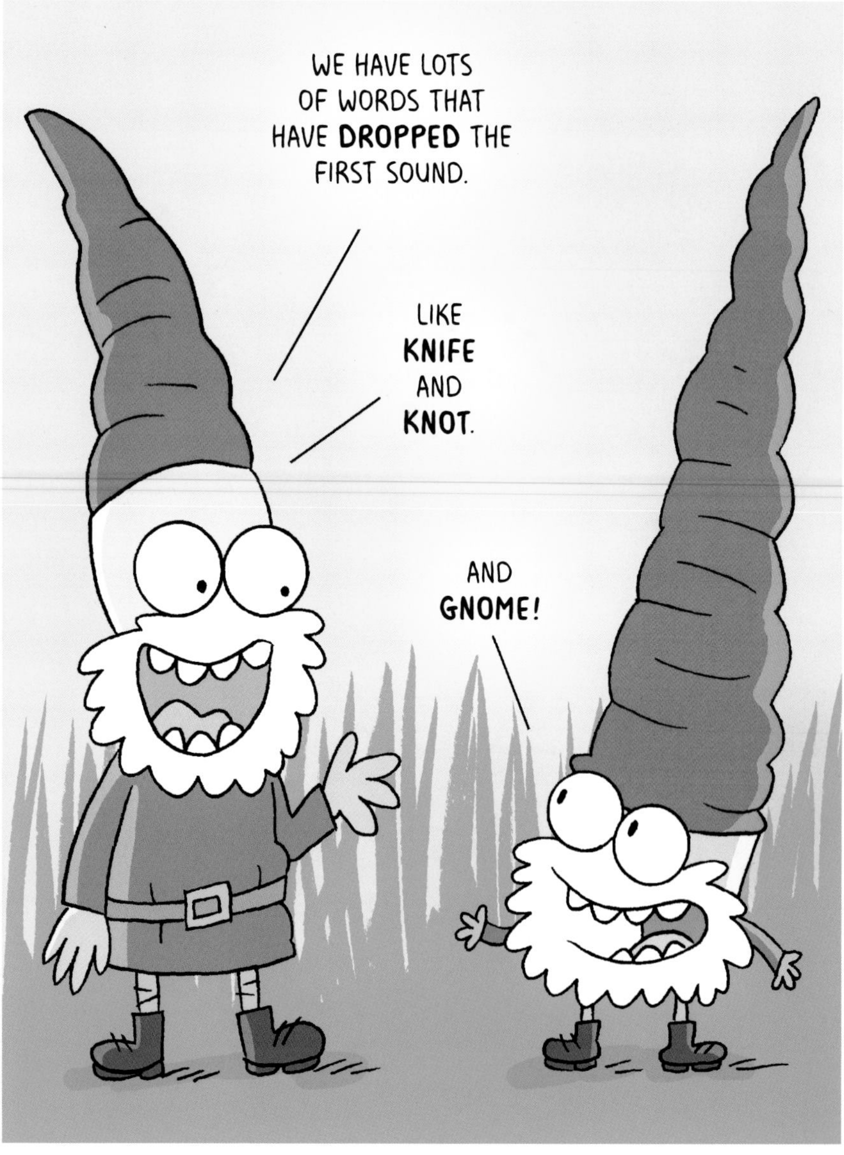

WE HAVE LOTS OF WORDS THAT HAVE **DROPPED** THE FIRST SOUND.
LIKE **KNIFE** AND **KNOT**.
AND **GNOME**!

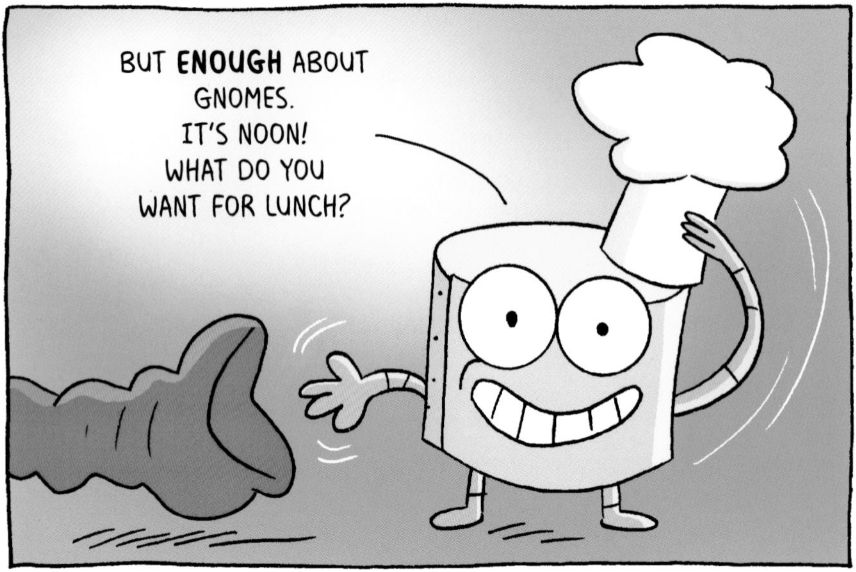
BUT **ENOUGH** ABOUT GNOMES.
IT'S NOON!
WHAT DO YOU WANT FOR LUNCH?

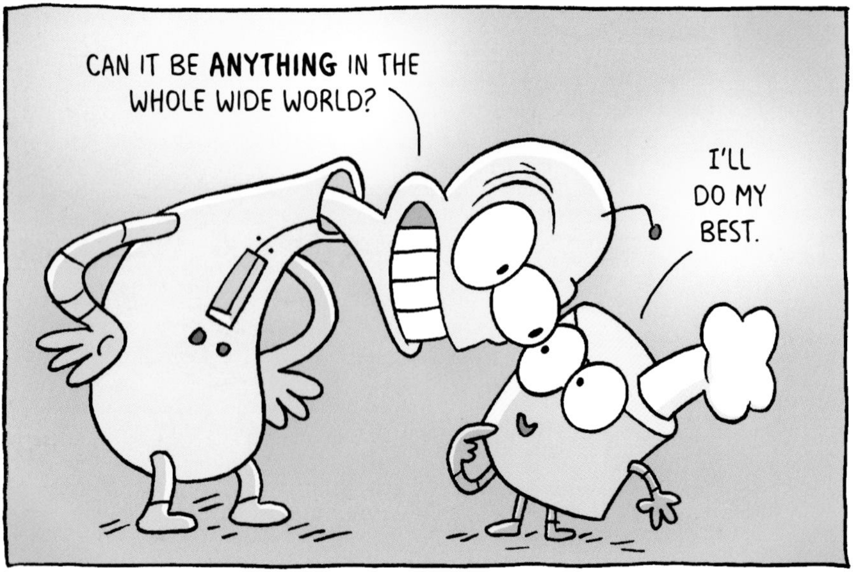
CAN IT BE **ANYTHING** IN THE WHOLE WIDE WORLD?
I'LL DO MY BEST.

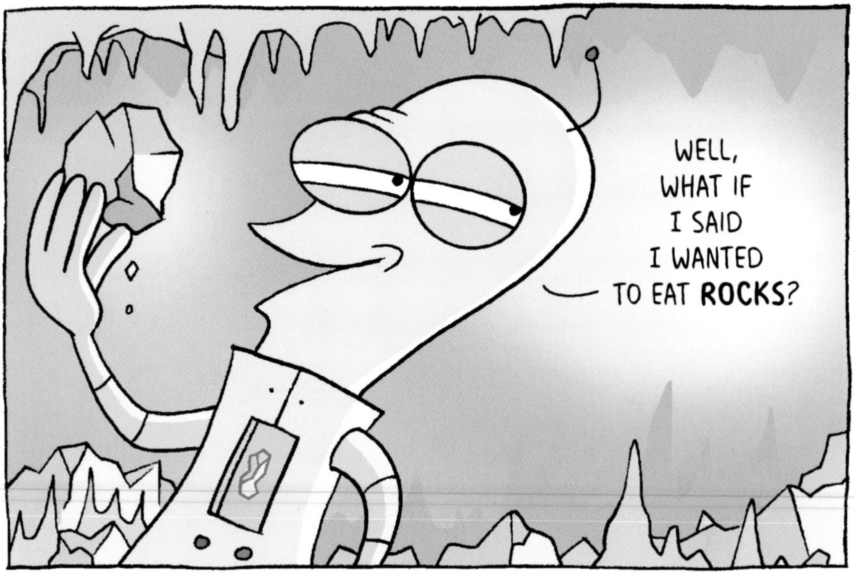
WELL, WHAT IF I SAID I WANTED TO EAT ROCKS?

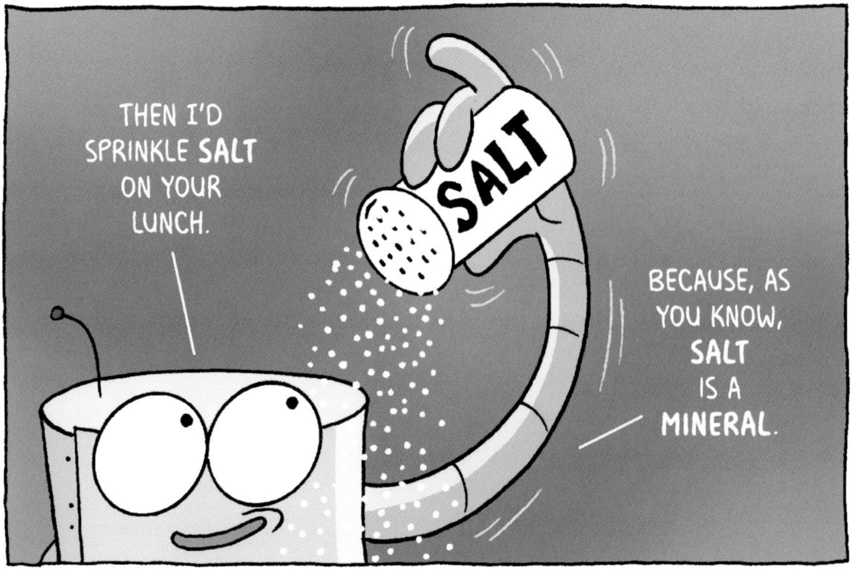
THEN I'D SPRINKLE SALT ON YOUR LUNCH.
SALT
BECAUSE, AS YOU KNOW, SALT IS A MINERAL.

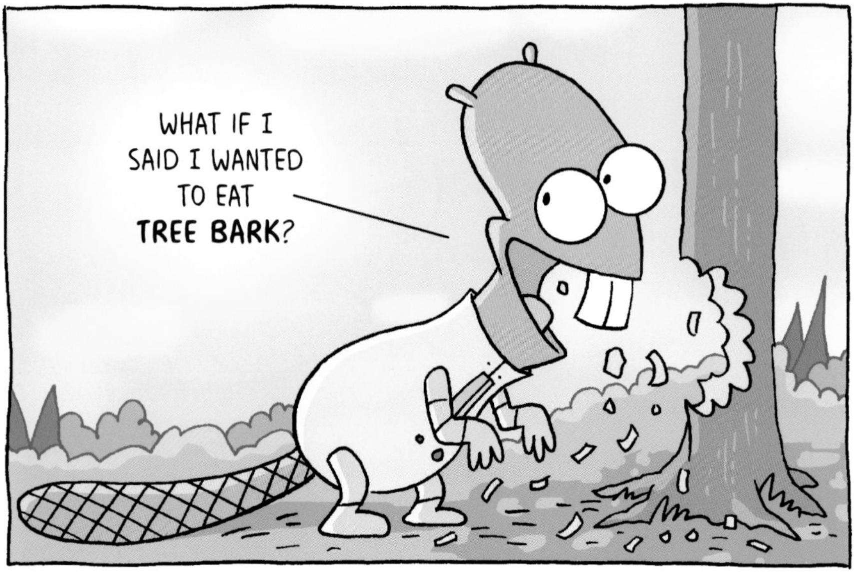
WHAT IF I SAID I WANTED TO EAT **TREE BARK**?

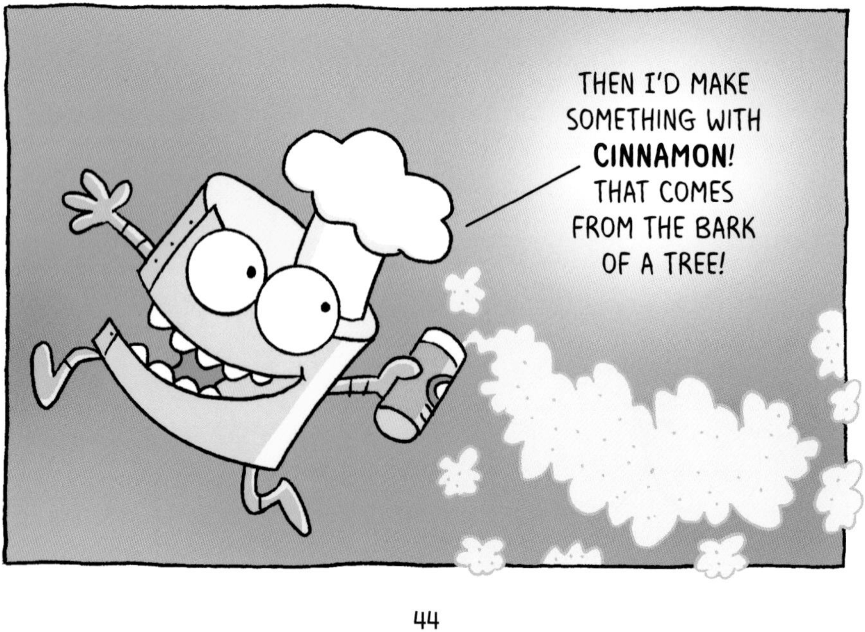
THEN I'D MAKE SOMETHING WITH **CINNAMON**! THAT COMES FROM THE BARK OF A TREE!

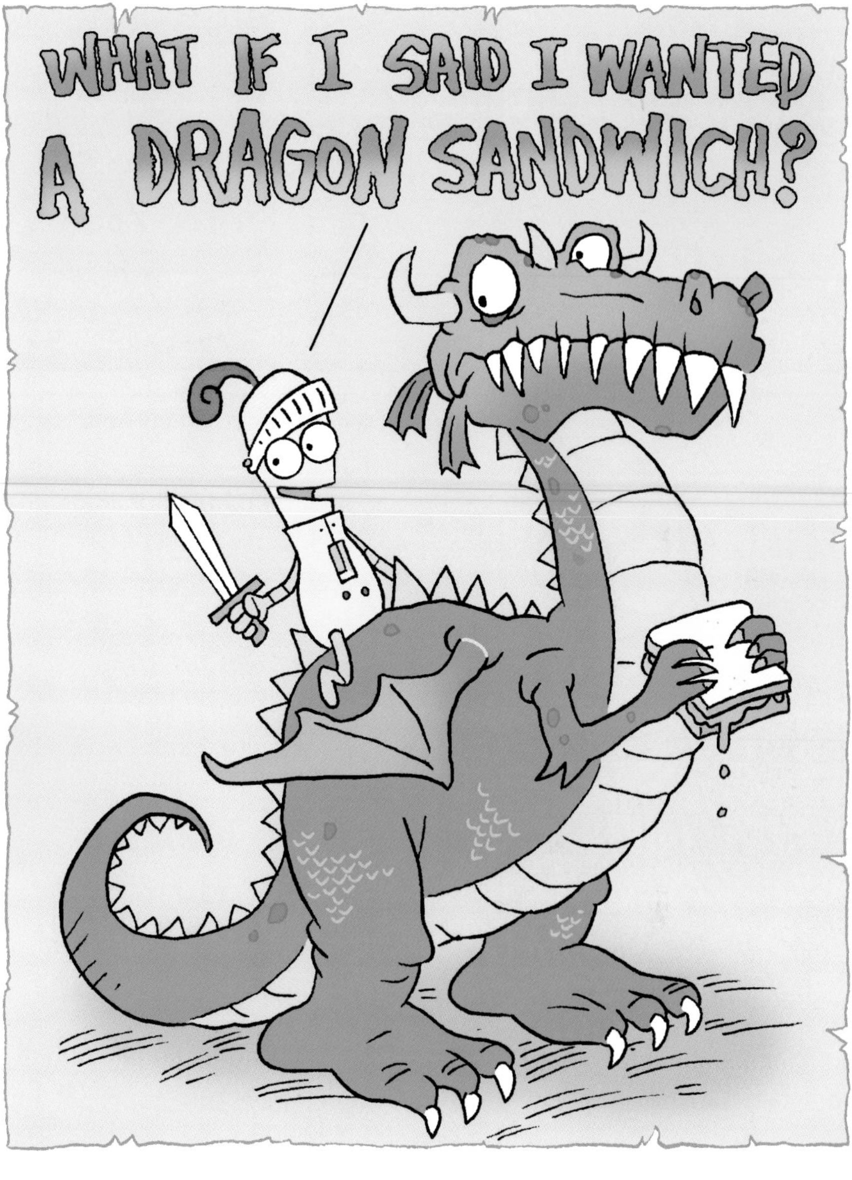
WHAT IF I SAID I WANTED A DRAGON SANDWICH?

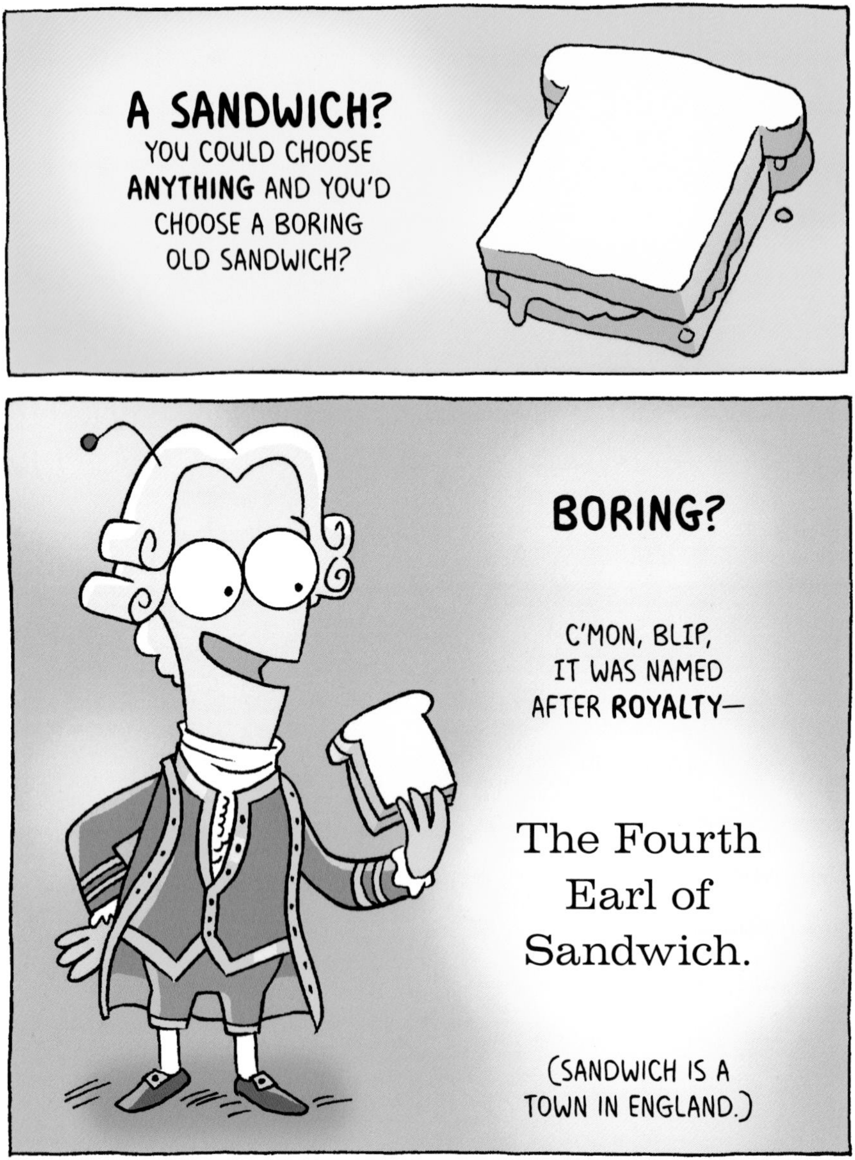
A SANDWICH?
YOU COULD CHOOSE **ANYTHING** AND YOU'D CHOOSE A BORING OLD SANDWICH?
BORING?
C'MON, BLIP, IT WAS NAMED AFTER **ROYALTY**—
The Fourth Earl of Sandwich.
(SANDWICH IS A TOWN IN ENGLAND.)

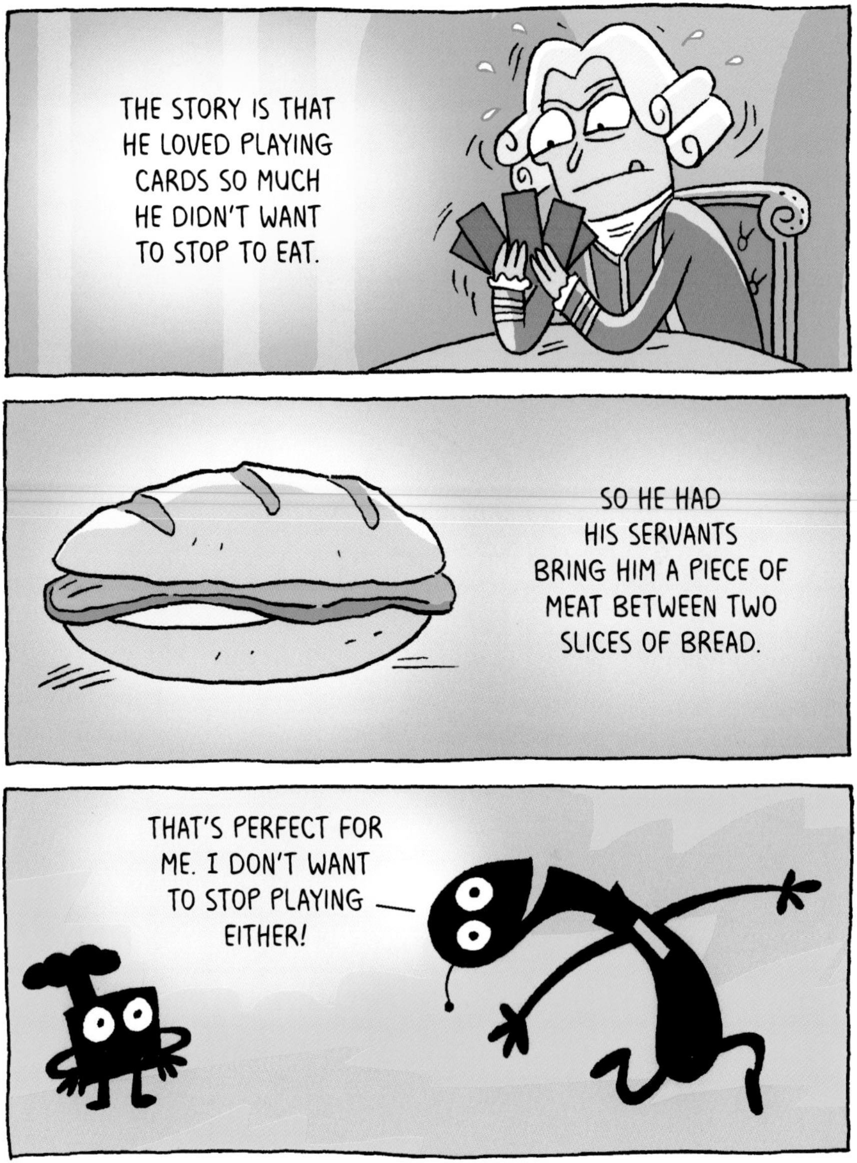
THE STORY IS THAT HE LOVED PLAYING CARDS SO MUCH HE DIDN'T WANT TO STOP TO EAT.
SO HE HAD HIS SERVANTS BRING HIM A PIECE OF MEAT BETWEEN TWO SLICES OF BREAD.
THAT'S PERFECT FOR ME. I DON'T WANT TO STOP PLAYING EITHER!

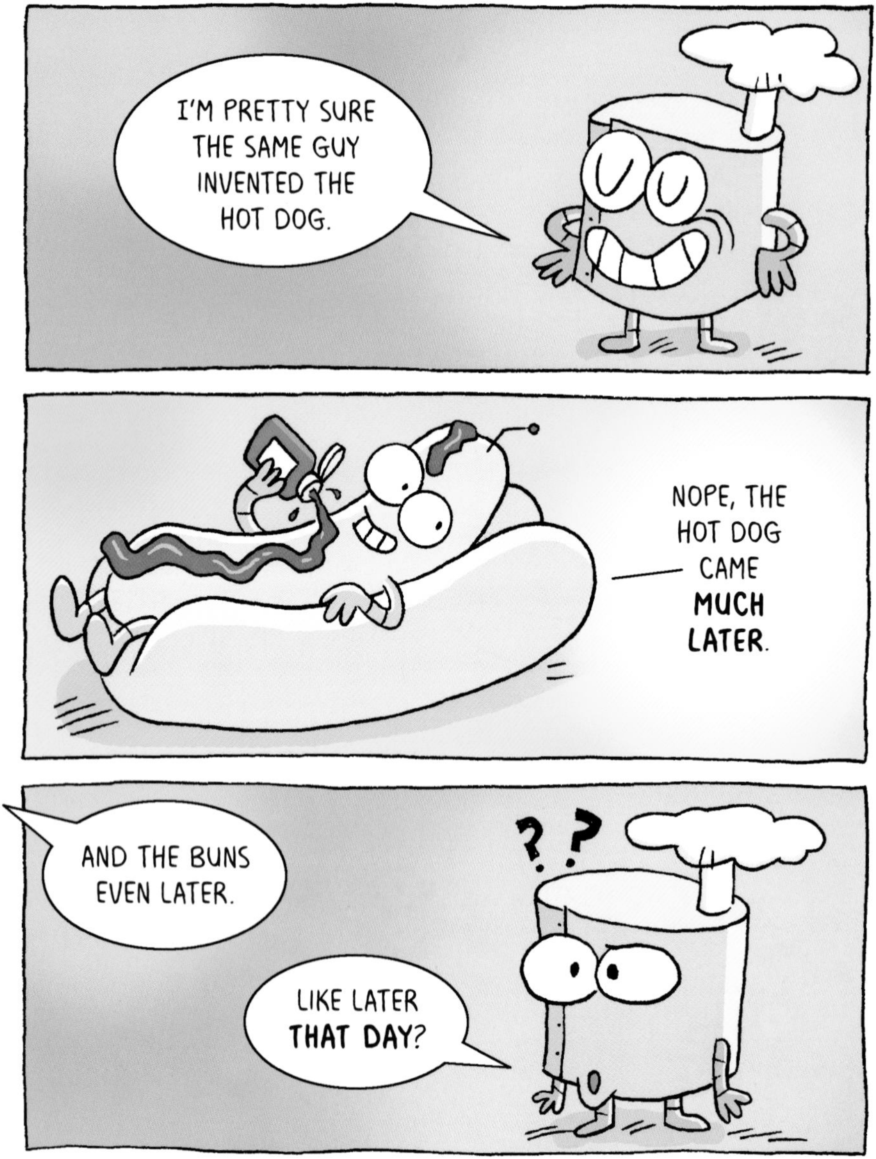
I'M PRETTY SURE THE SAME GUY INVENTED THE HOT DOG.
NOPE, THE HOT DOG CAME **MUCH LATER**.
AND THE BUNS EVEN LATER.
??
LIKE LATER **THAT DAY**?

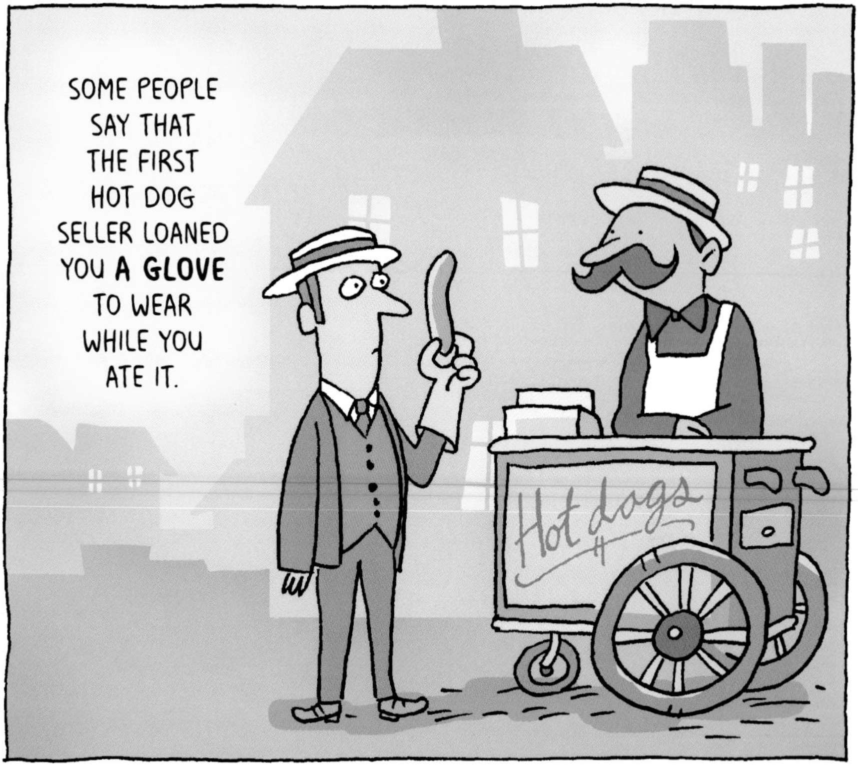
SOME PEOPLE SAY THAT THE FIRST HOT DOG SELLER LOANED YOU **A GLOVE** TO WEAR WHILE YOU ATE IT.
Hot dogs

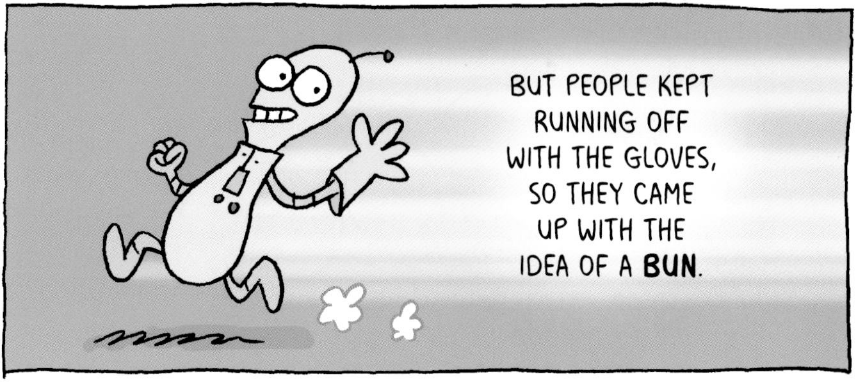
BUT PEOPLE KEPT RUNNING OFF WITH THE GLOVES, SO THEY CAME UP WITH THE IDEA OF A **BUN**.

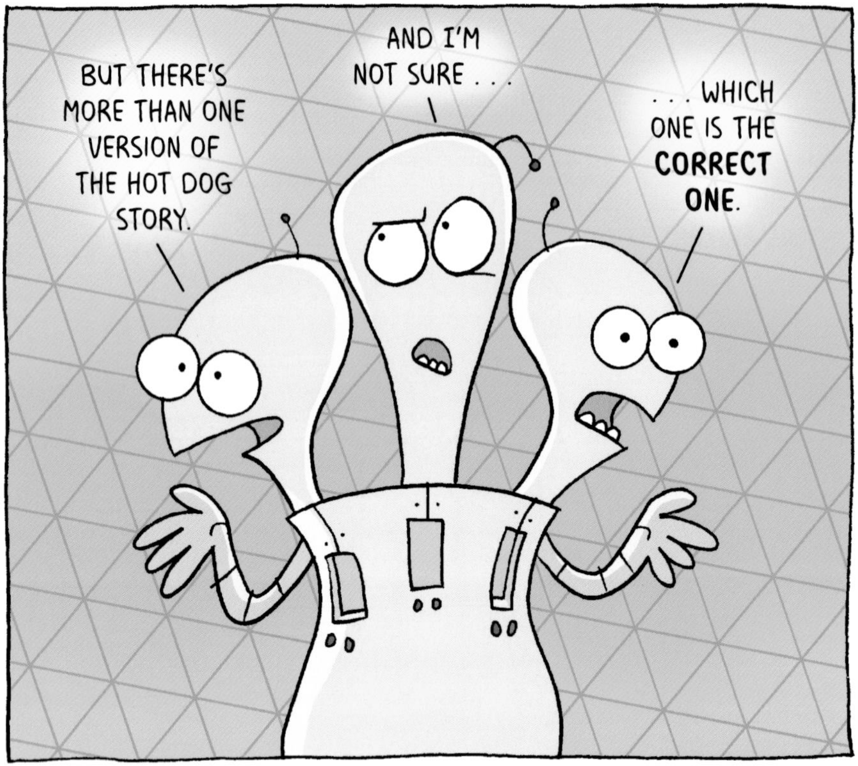
BUT THERE'S MORE THAN ONE VERSION OF THE HOT DOG STORY.
AND I'M NOT SURE . . .
. . . WHICH ONE IS THE **CORRECT ONE**.

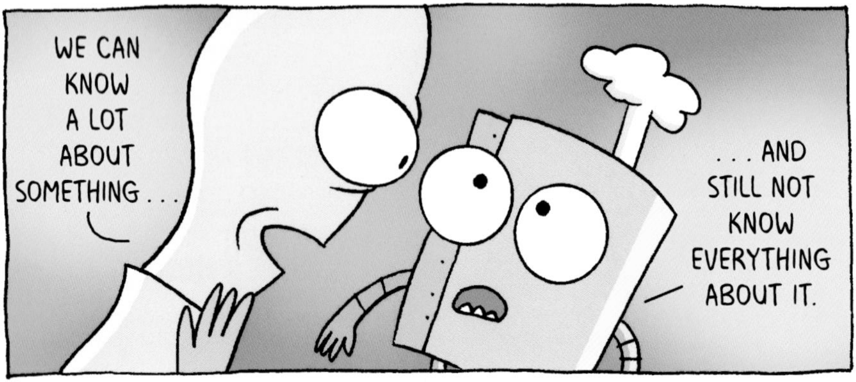
WE CAN KNOW A LOT ABOUT SOMETHING . . .
. . . AND STILL NOT KNOW EVERYTHING ABOUT IT.

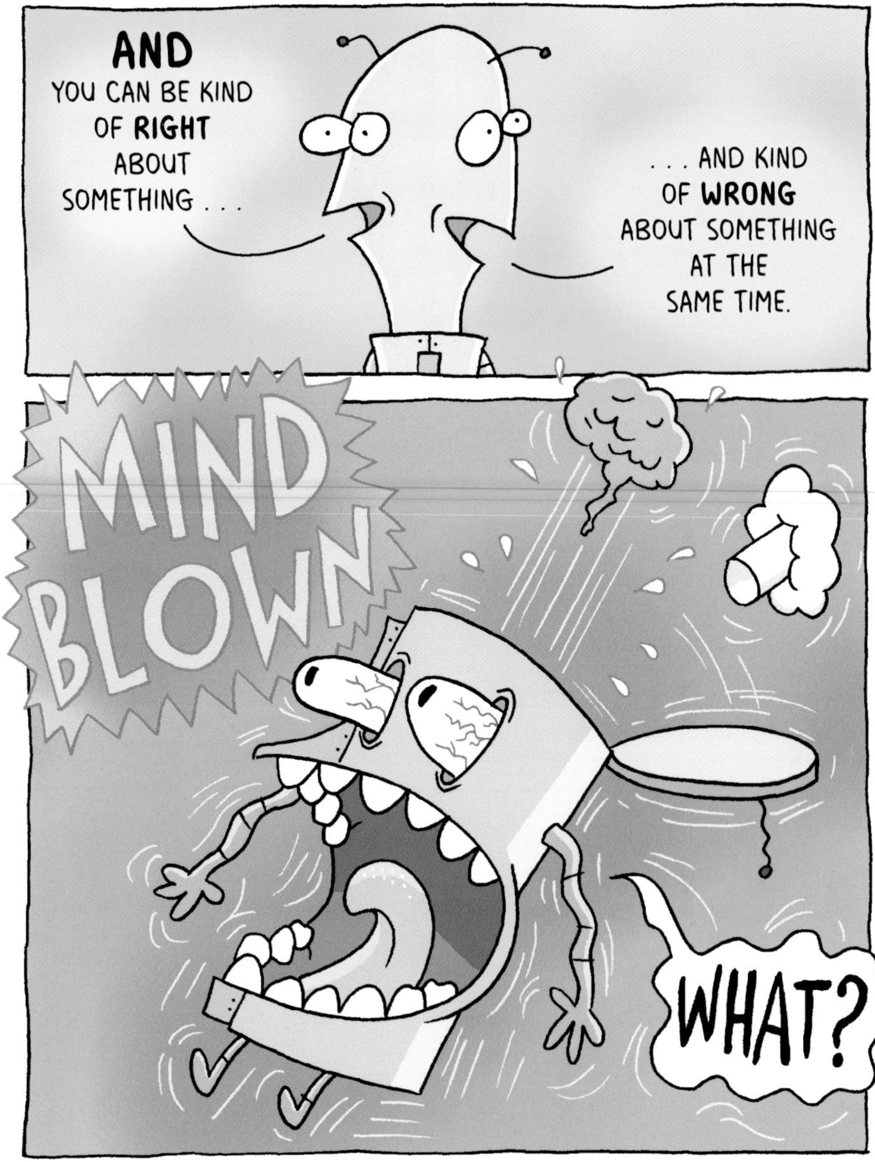
AND
YOU CAN BE KIND OF RIGHT ABOUT SOMETHING . . .
. . . AND KIND OF WRONG ABOUT SOMETHING AT THE SAME TIME.
MIND BLOWN
WHAT?

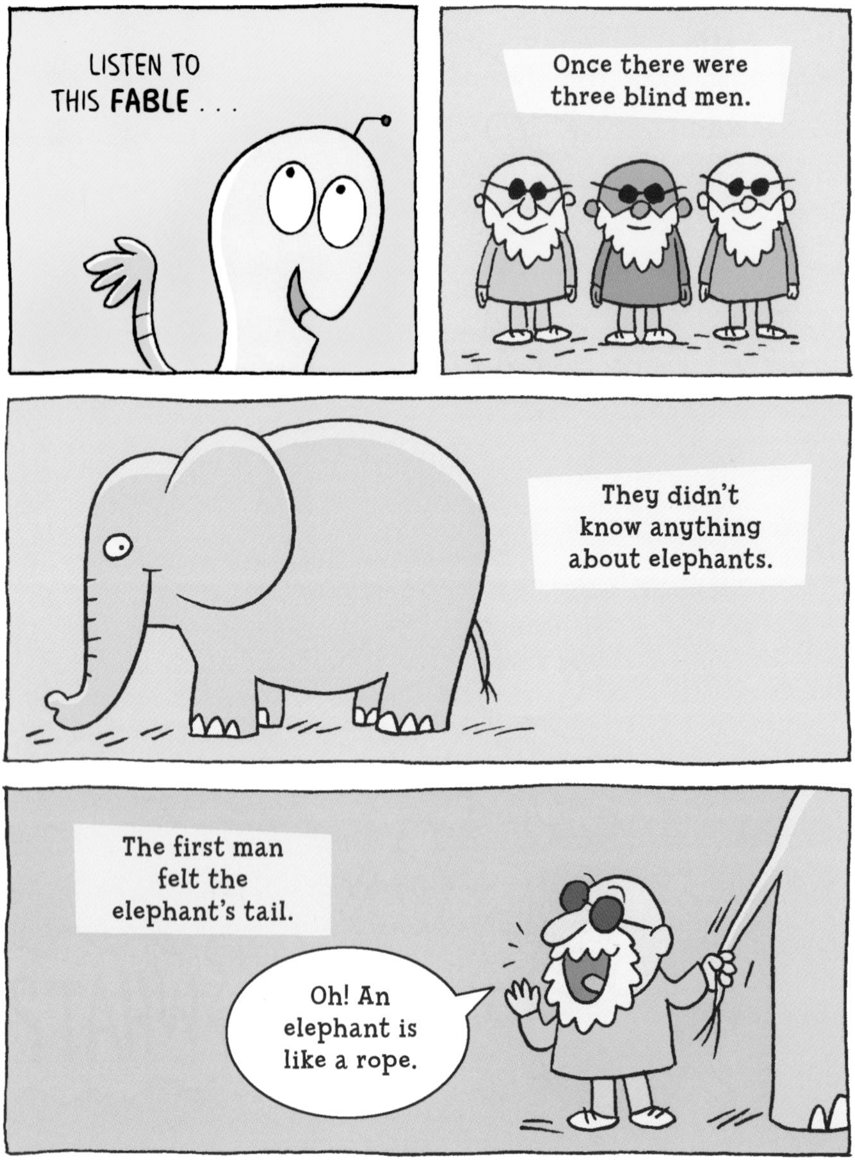
LISTEN TO
THIS FABLE . . .
Once there were three blind men.
They didn't know anything about elephants.
The first man felt the elephant's tail.
Oh! An elephant is like a rope.

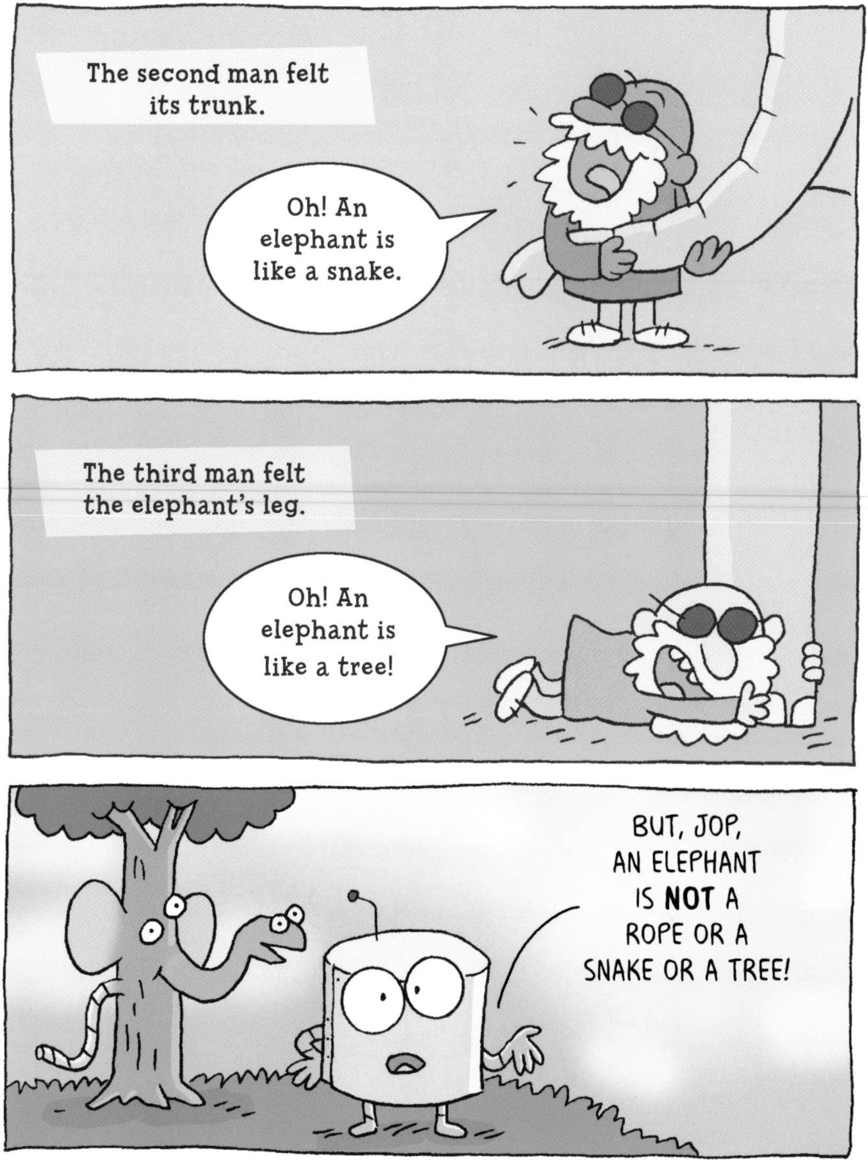
The second man felt its trunk.
Oh! An elephant is like a snake.
The third man felt the elephant's leg.
Oh! An elephant is like a tree!
BUT, JOP, AN ELEPHANT IS **NOT** A ROPE OR A SNAKE OR A TREE!

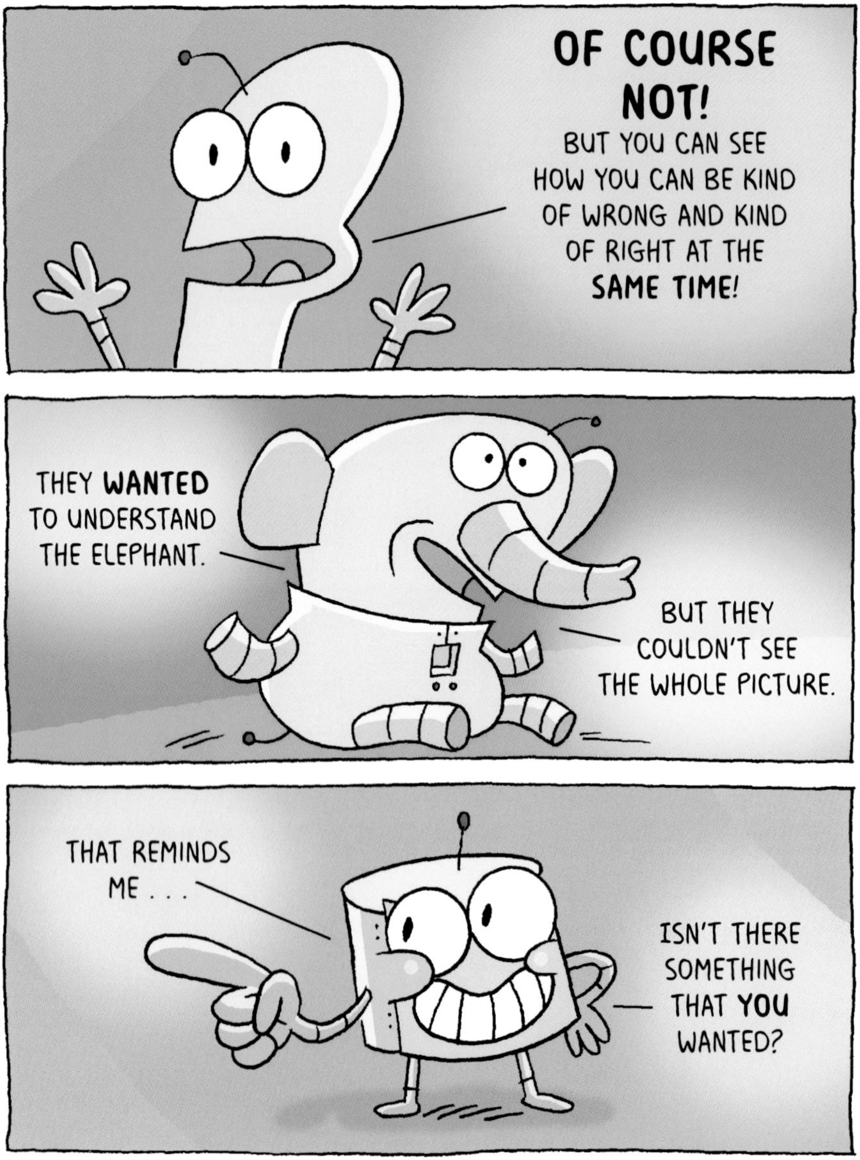
OF COURSE NOT!
BUT YOU CAN SEE HOW YOU CAN BE KIND OF WRONG AND KIND OF RIGHT AT THE **SAME TIME!**
THEY **WANTED** TO UNDERSTAND THE ELEPHANT.
BUT THEY COULDN'T SEE THE WHOLE PICTURE.
THAT REMINDS ME . . .
ISN'T THERE SOMETHING THAT **YOU** WANTED?

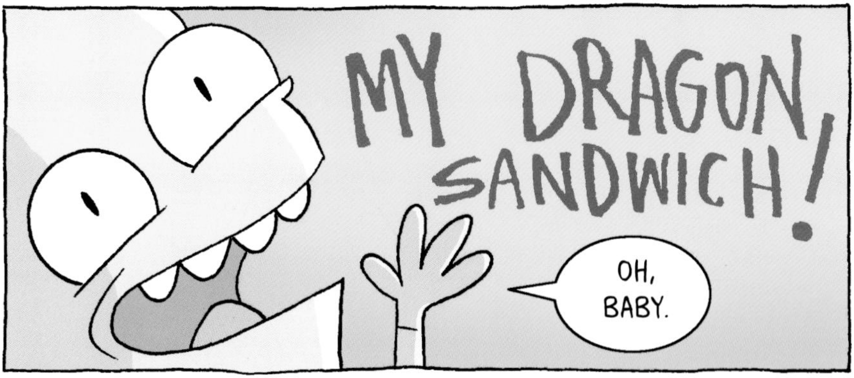
MY DRAGON SANDWICH!
OH, BABY.

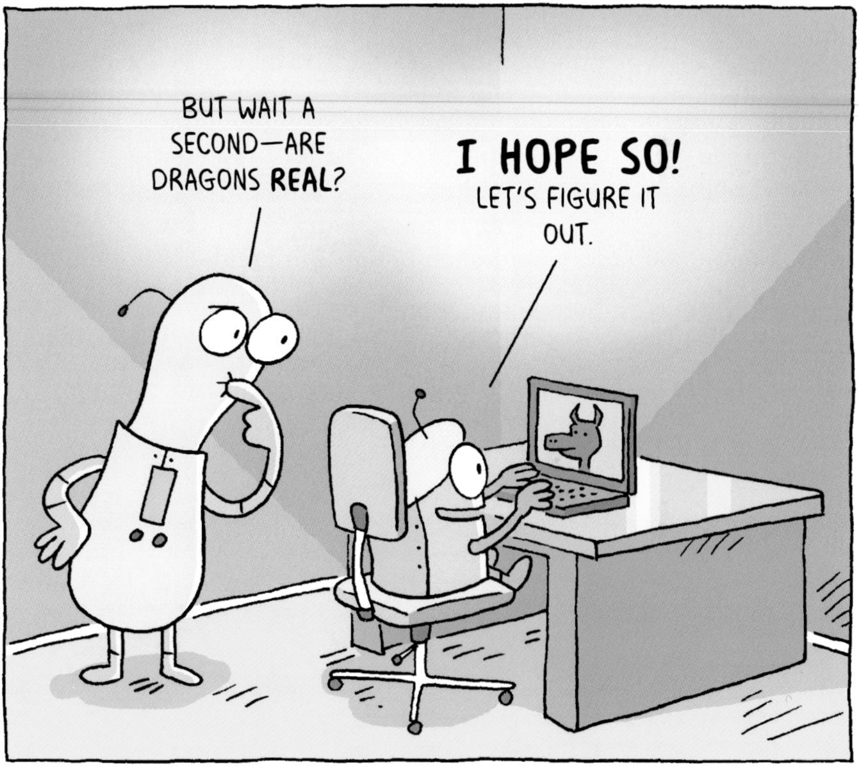
BUT WAIT A SECOND—ARE DRAGONS **REAL**?
I HOPE SO! LET'S FIGURE IT OUT.

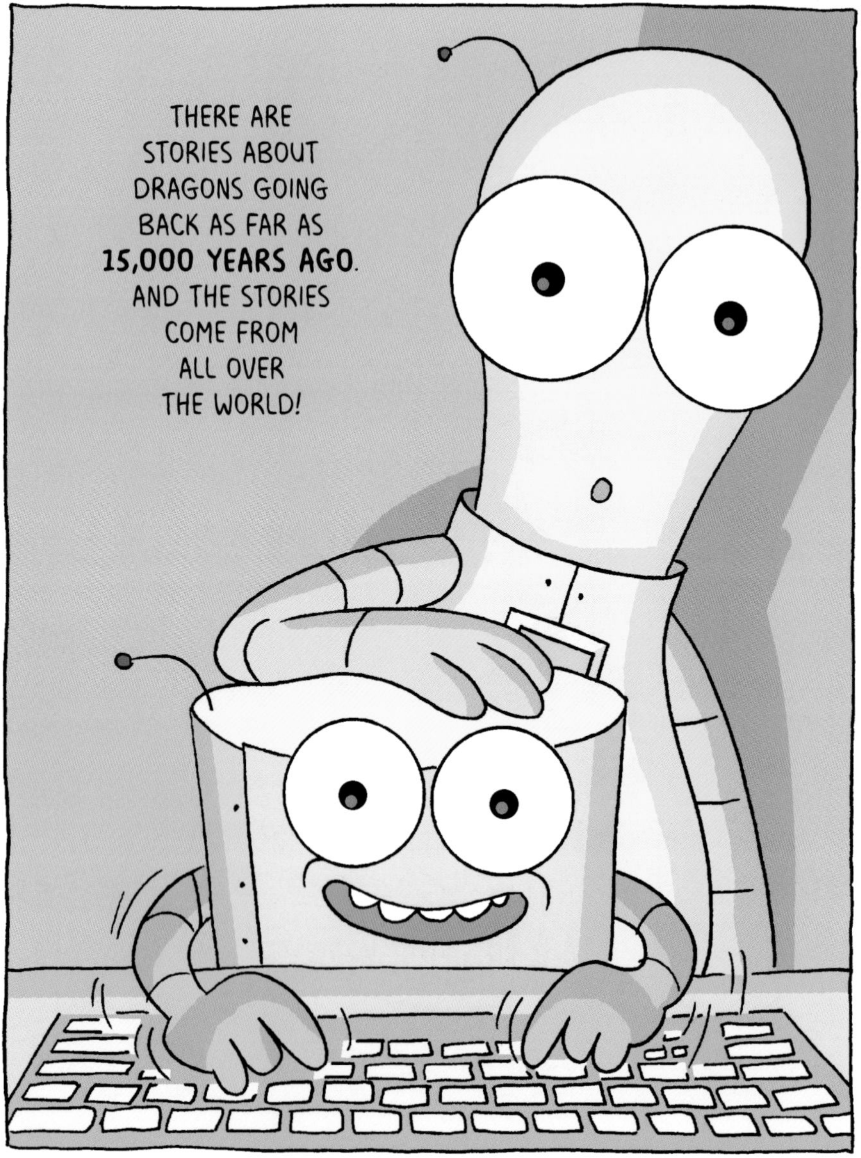
THERE ARE STORIES ABOUT DRAGONS GOING BACK AS FAR AS **15,000 YEARS AGO**. AND THE STORIES COME FROM ALL OVER THE WORLD!

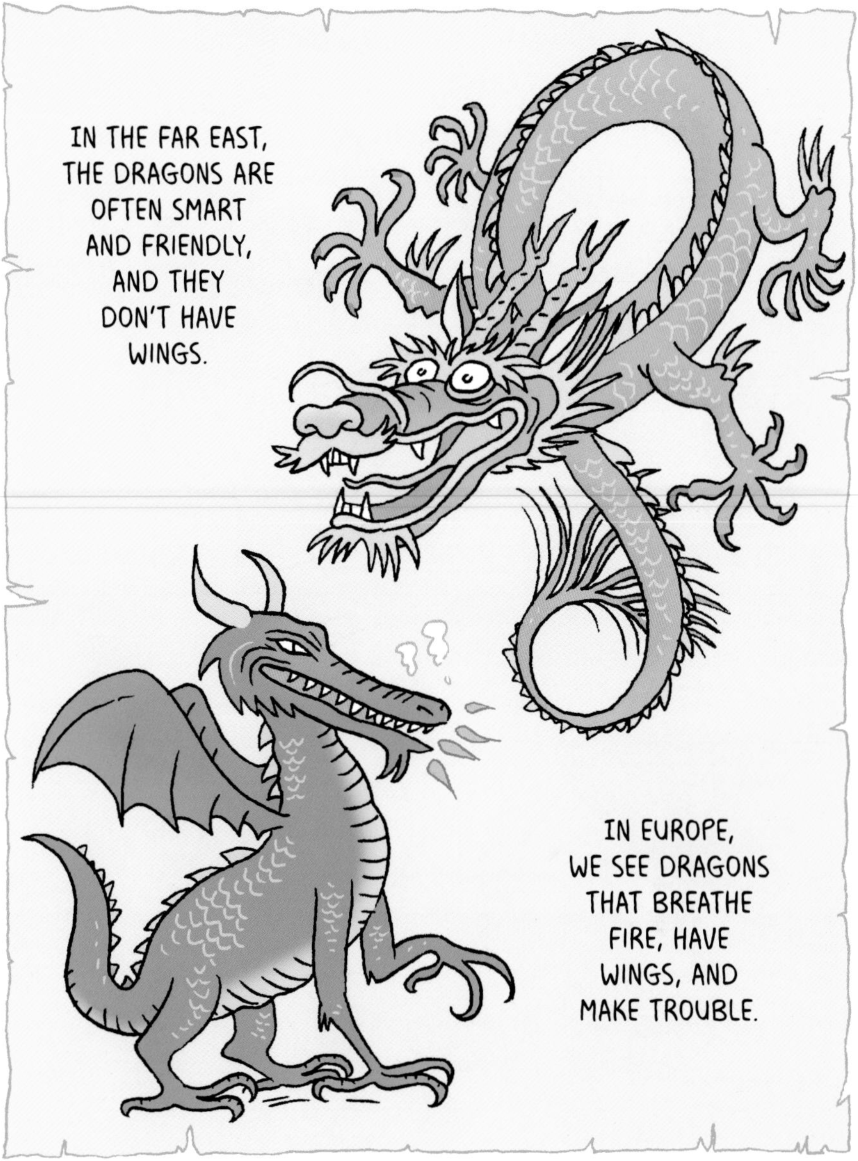
IN THE FAR EAST, THE DRAGONS ARE OFTEN SMART AND FRIENDLY, AND THEY DON'T HAVE WINGS.
IN EUROPE, WE SEE DRAGONS THAT BREATHE FIRE, HAVE WINGS, AND MAKE TROUBLE.

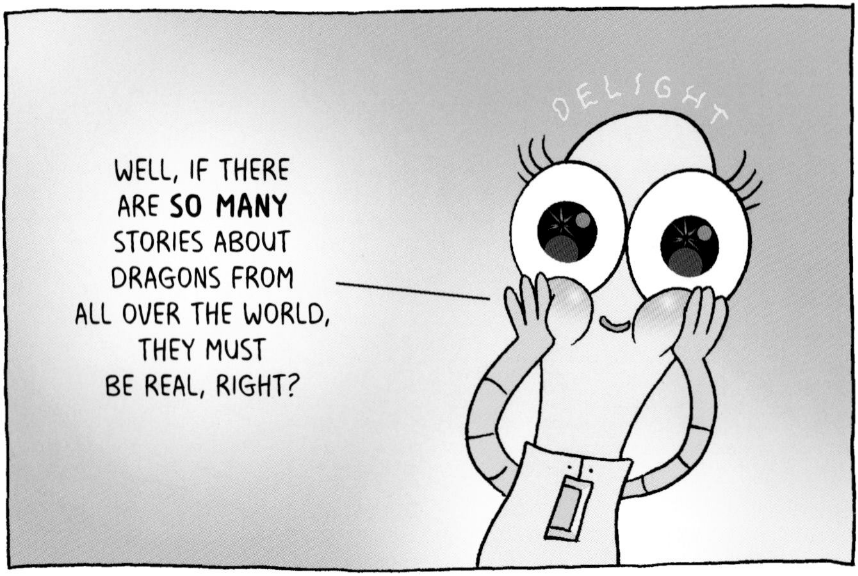
DELIGHT
WELL, IF THERE ARE **SO MANY** STORIES ABOUT DRAGONS FROM ALL OVER THE WORLD, THEY MUST BE REAL, RIGHT?

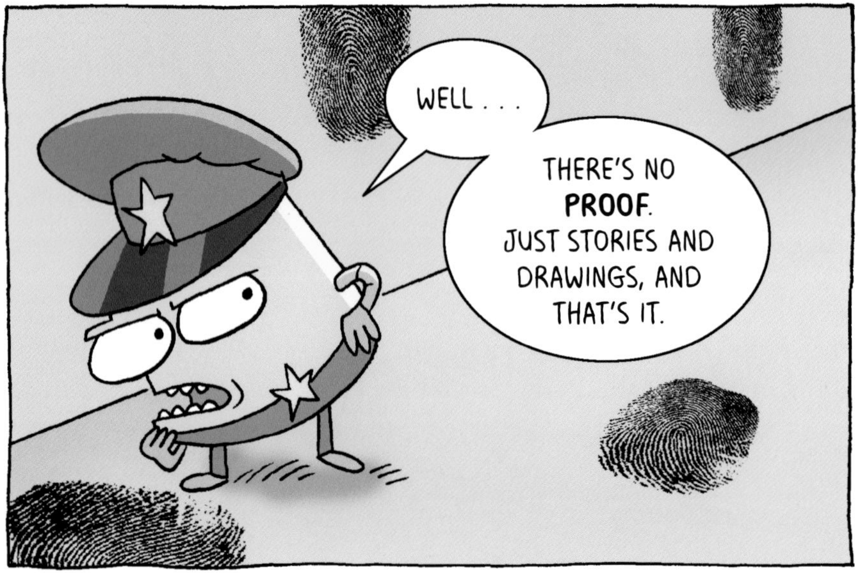
WELL . . .
THERE'S NO **PROOF**. JUST STORIES AND DRAWINGS, AND THAT'S IT.

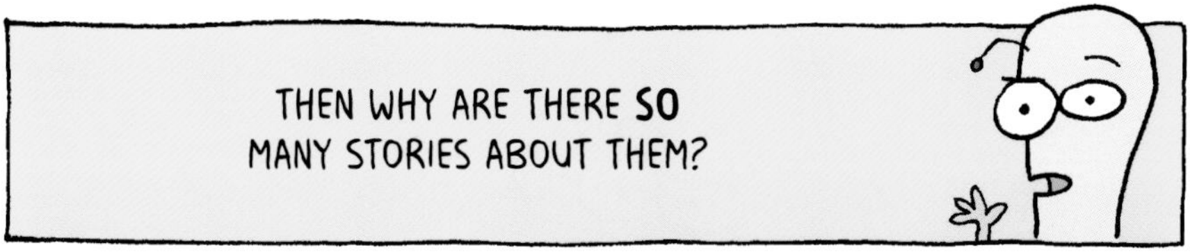
THEN WHY ARE THERE SO MANY STORIES ABOUT THEM?

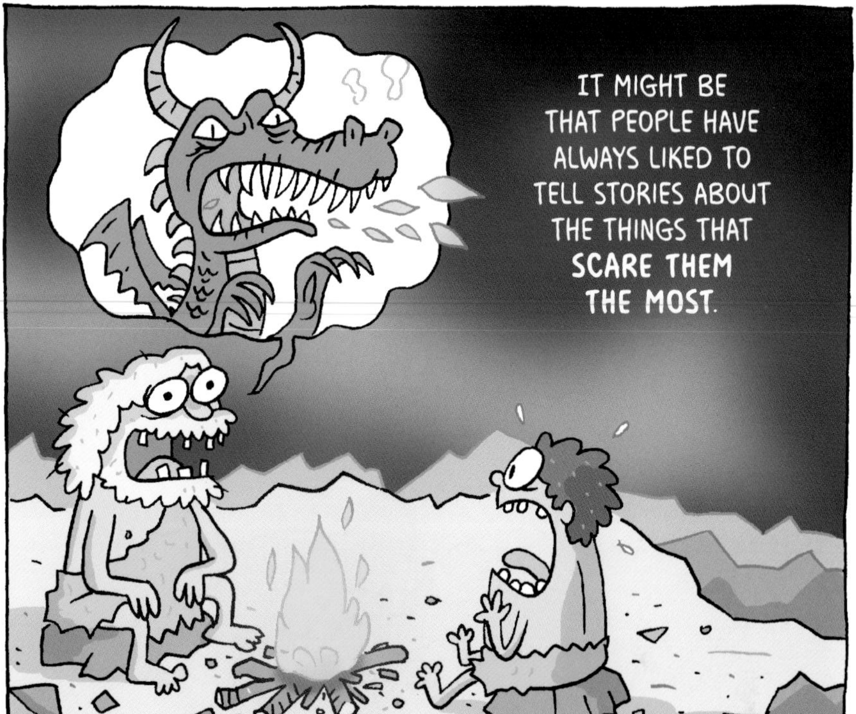
IT MIGHT BE THAT PEOPLE HAVE ALWAYS LIKED TO TELL STORIES ABOUT THE THINGS THAT SCARE THEM THE MOST.

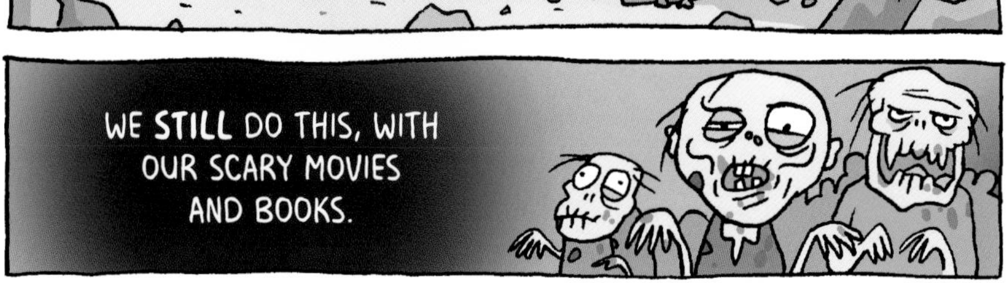
WE STILL DO THIS, WITH OUR SCARY MOVIES AND BOOKS.

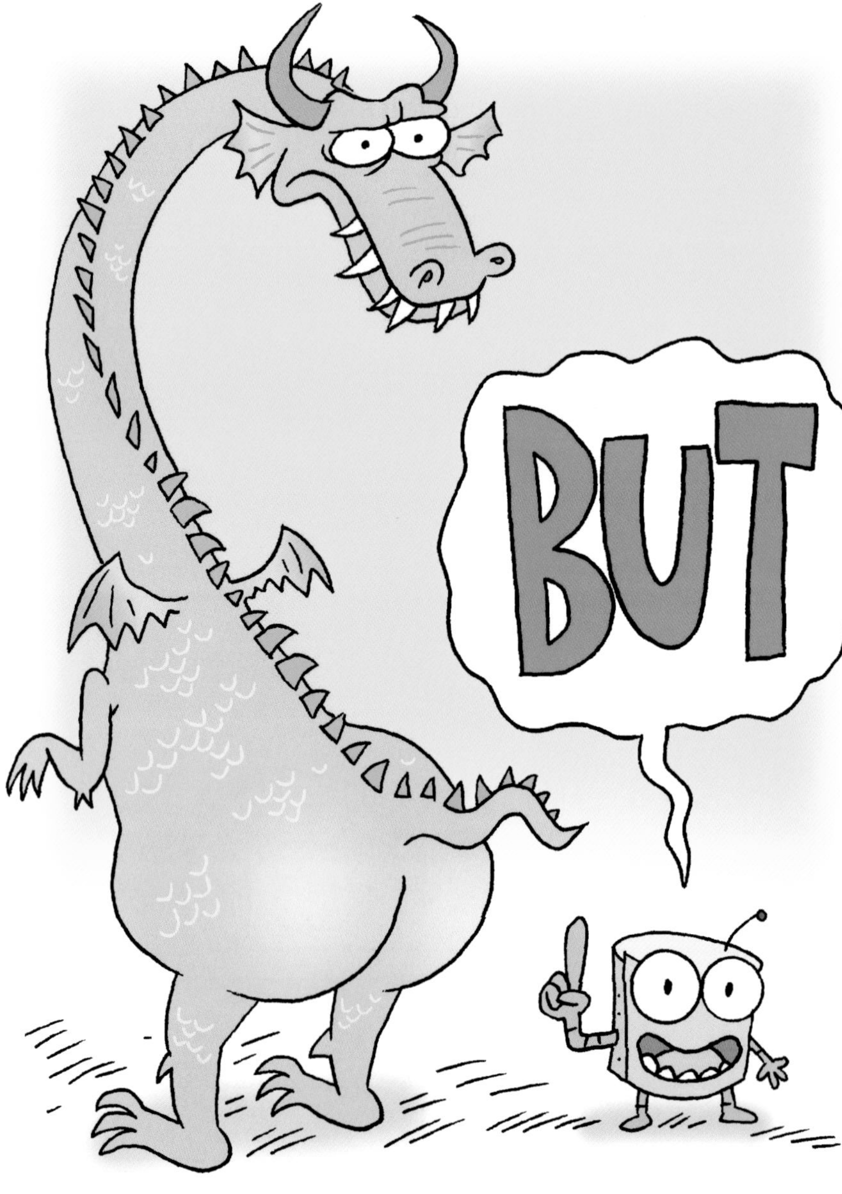
BUT

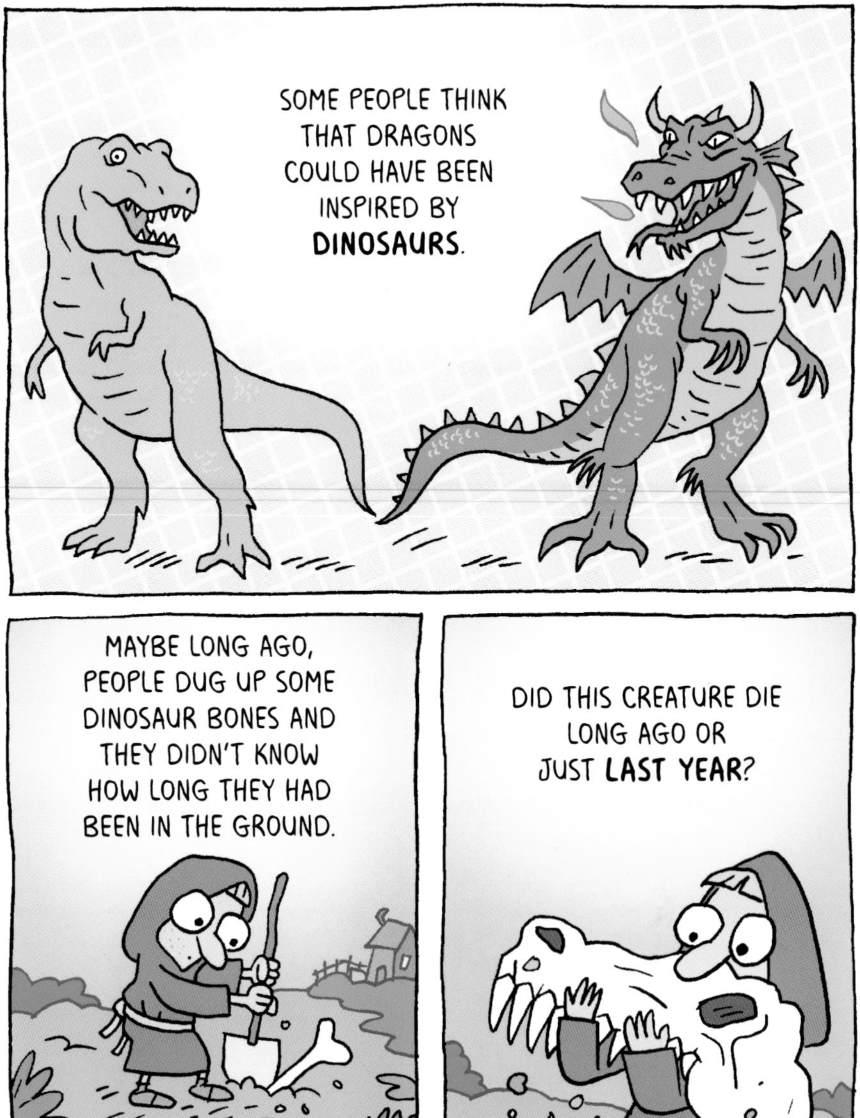
SOME PEOPLE THINK THAT DRAGONS COULD HAVE BEEN INSPIRED BY **DINOSAURS**.
MAYBE LONG AGO, PEOPLE DUG UP SOME DINOSAUR BONES AND THEY DIDN'T KNOW HOW LONG THEY HAD BEEN IN THE GROUND.
DID THIS CREATURE DIE LONG AGO OR JUST **LAST YEAR**?

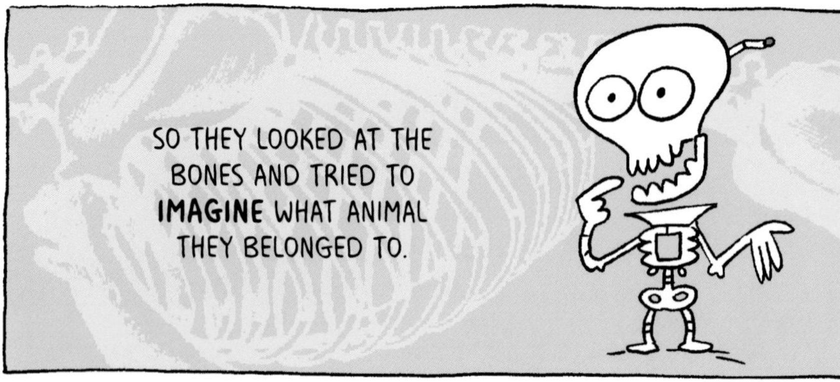
SO THEY LOOKED AT THE BONES AND TRIED TO **IMAGINE** WHAT ANIMAL THEY BELONGED TO.

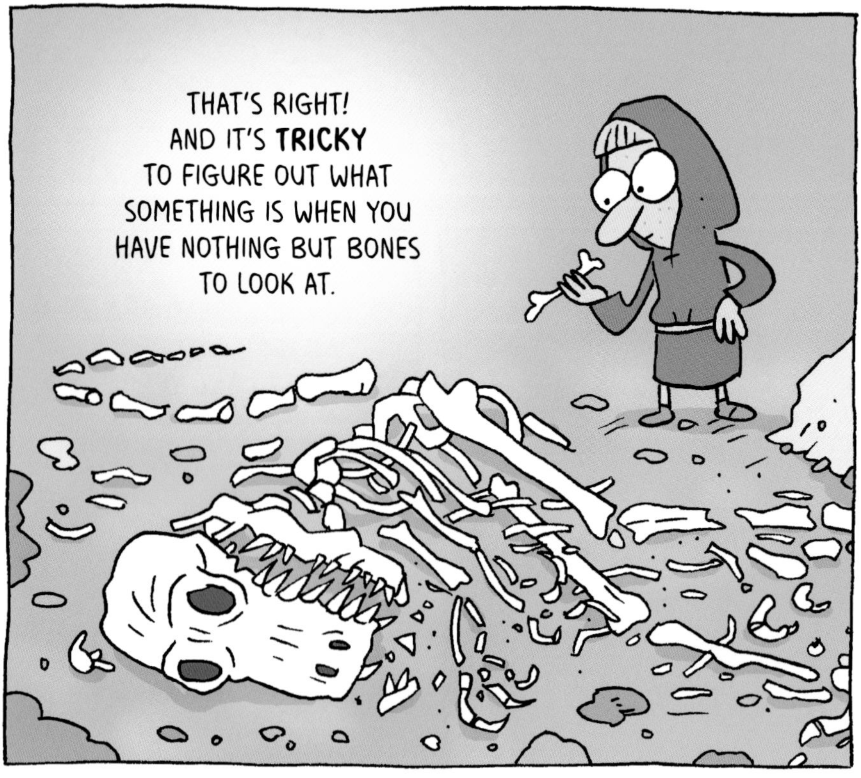
THAT'S RIGHT! AND IT'S **TRICKY** TO FIGURE OUT WHAT SOMETHING IS WHEN YOU HAVE NOTHING BUT BONES TO LOOK AT.

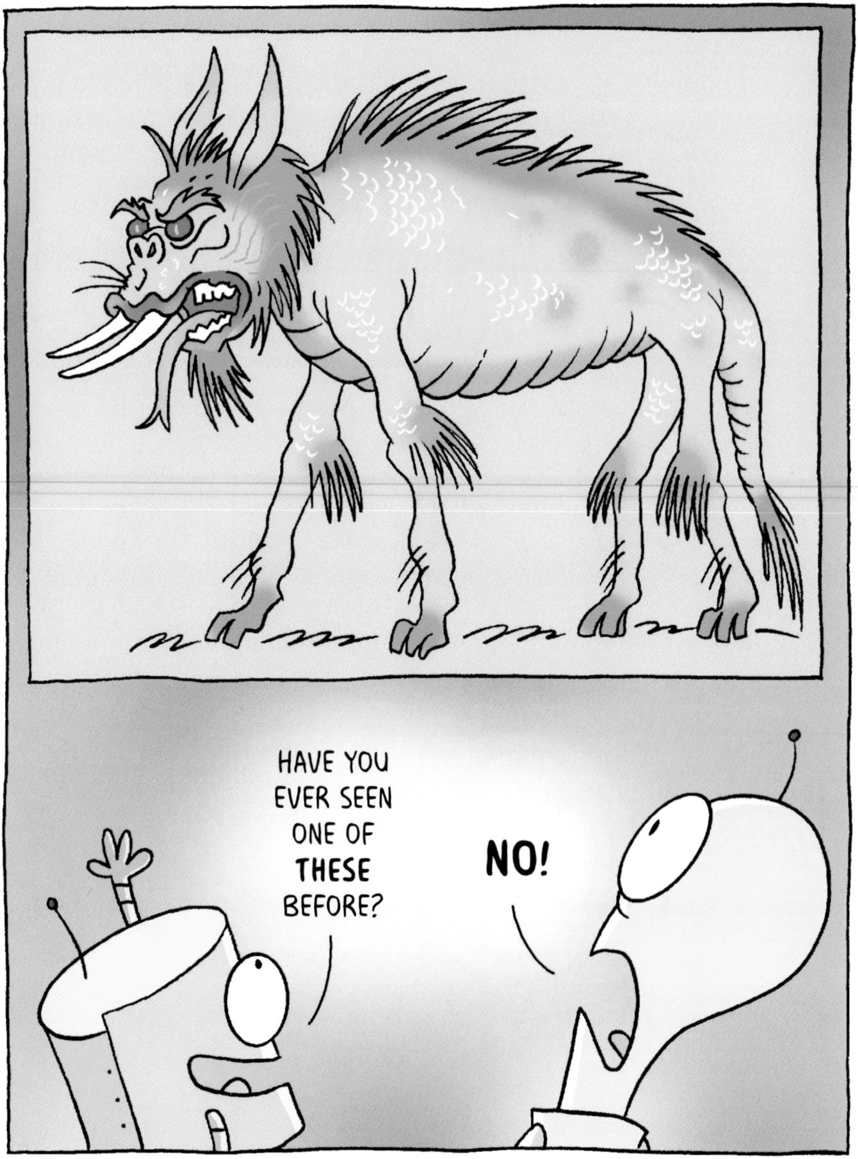
HAVE YOU EVER SEEN ONE OF **THESE** BEFORE?
NO!

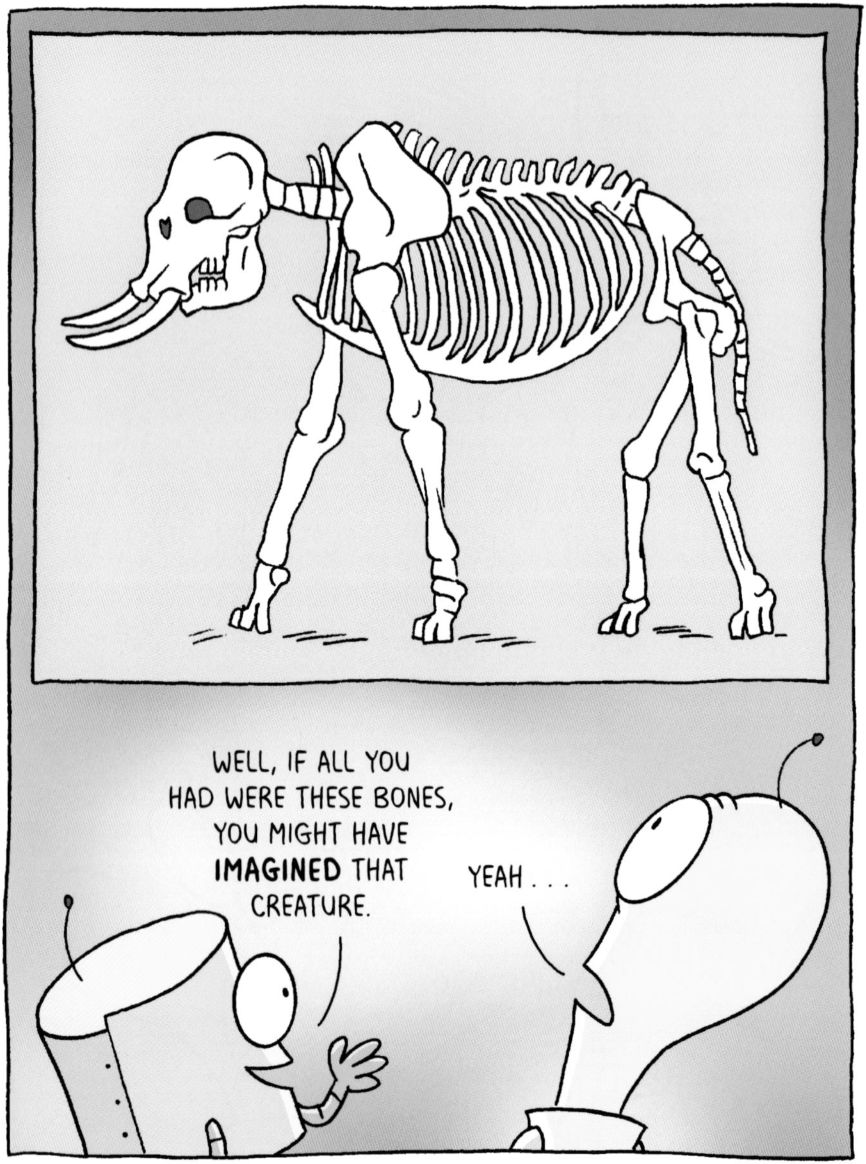
WELL, IF ALL YOU HAD WERE THESE BONES, YOU MIGHT HAVE **IMAGINED** THAT CREATURE.
YEAH . . .

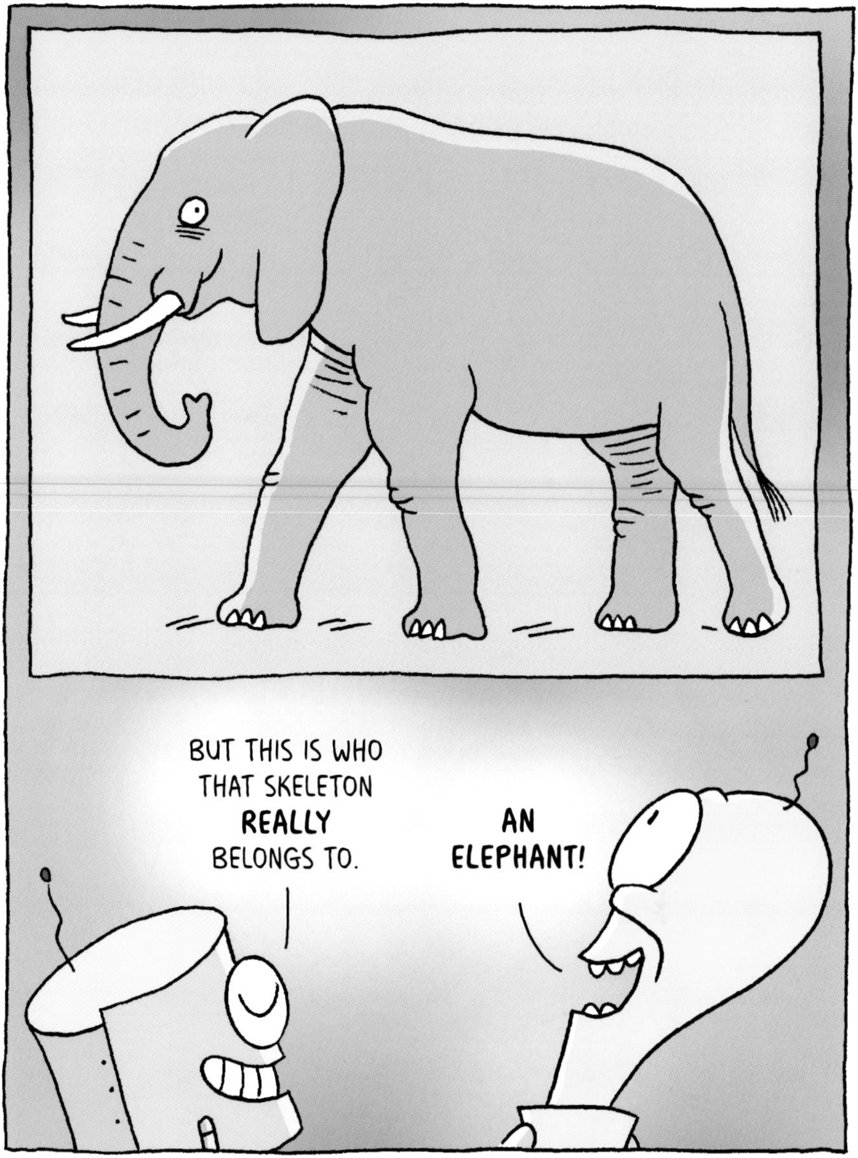
BUT THIS IS WHO THAT SKELETON **REALLY** BELONGS TO.
AN ELEPHANT!

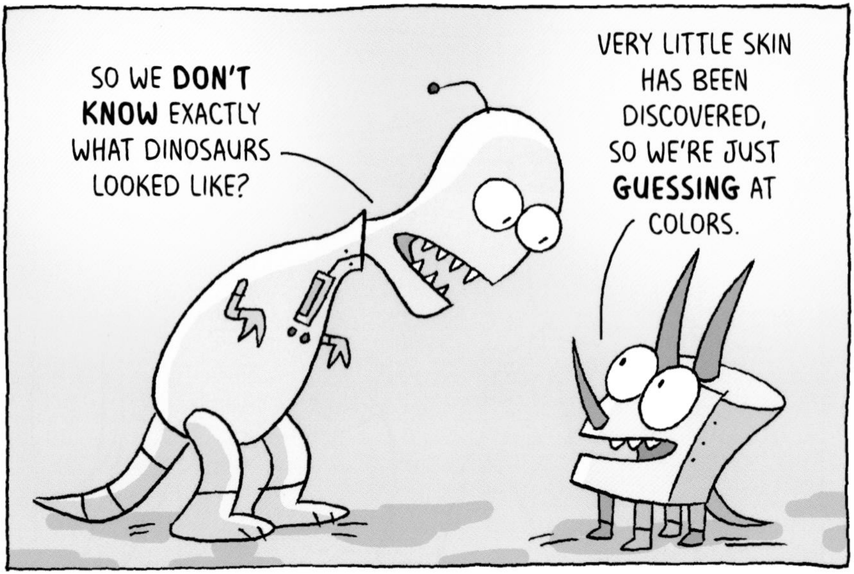
SO WE **DON'T KNOW** EXACTLY WHAT DINOSAURS LOOKED LIKE?
VERY LITTLE SKIN HAS BEEN DISCOVERED, SO WE'RE JUST **GUESSING** AT COLORS.

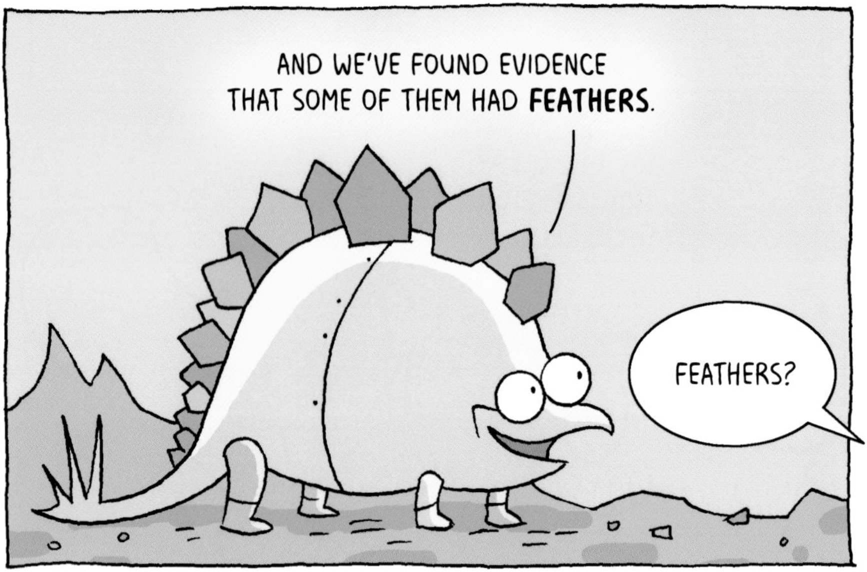
AND WE'VE FOUND EVIDENCE THAT SOME OF THEM HAD **FEATHERS**.
FEATHERS?

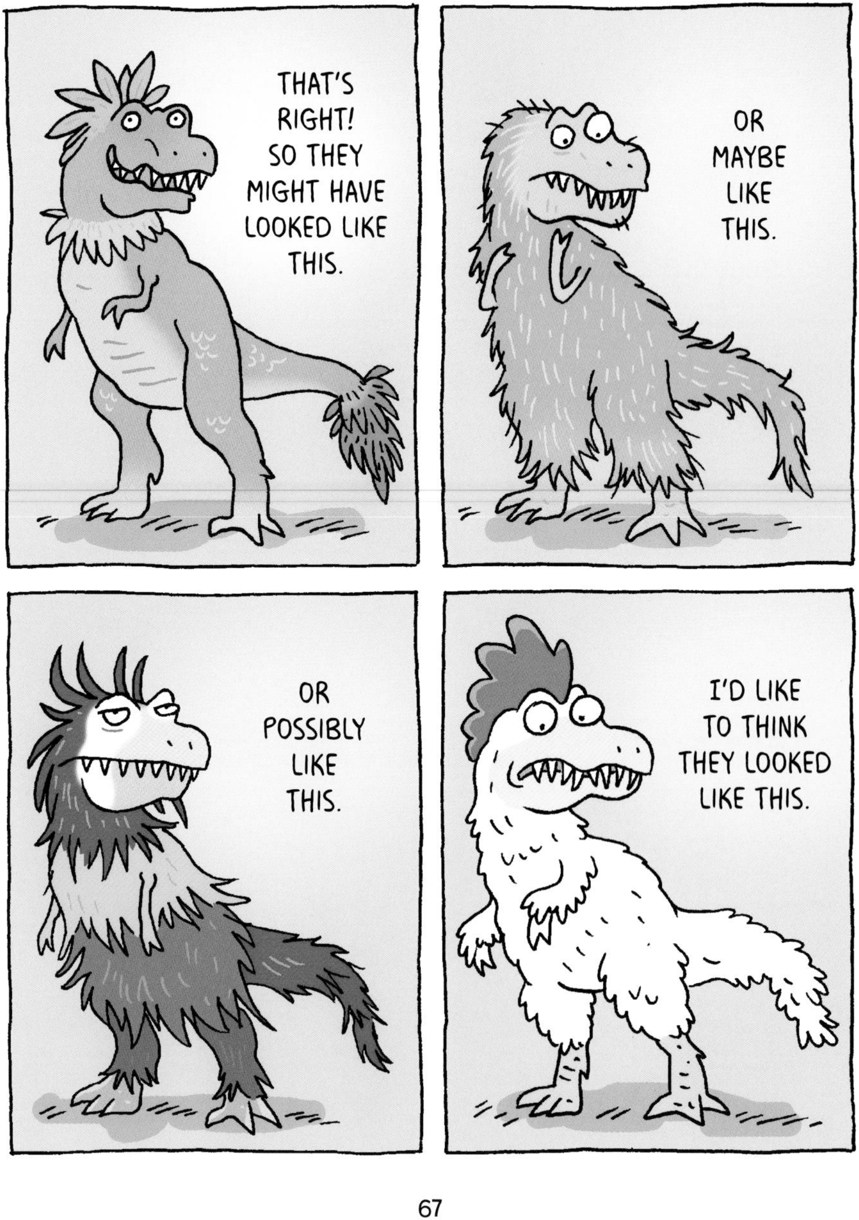
THAT'S RIGHT! SO THEY MIGHT HAVE LOOKED LIKE THIS.
OR MAYBE LIKE THIS.
OR POSSIBLY LIKE THIS.
I'D LIKE TO THINK THEY LOOKED LIKE THIS.

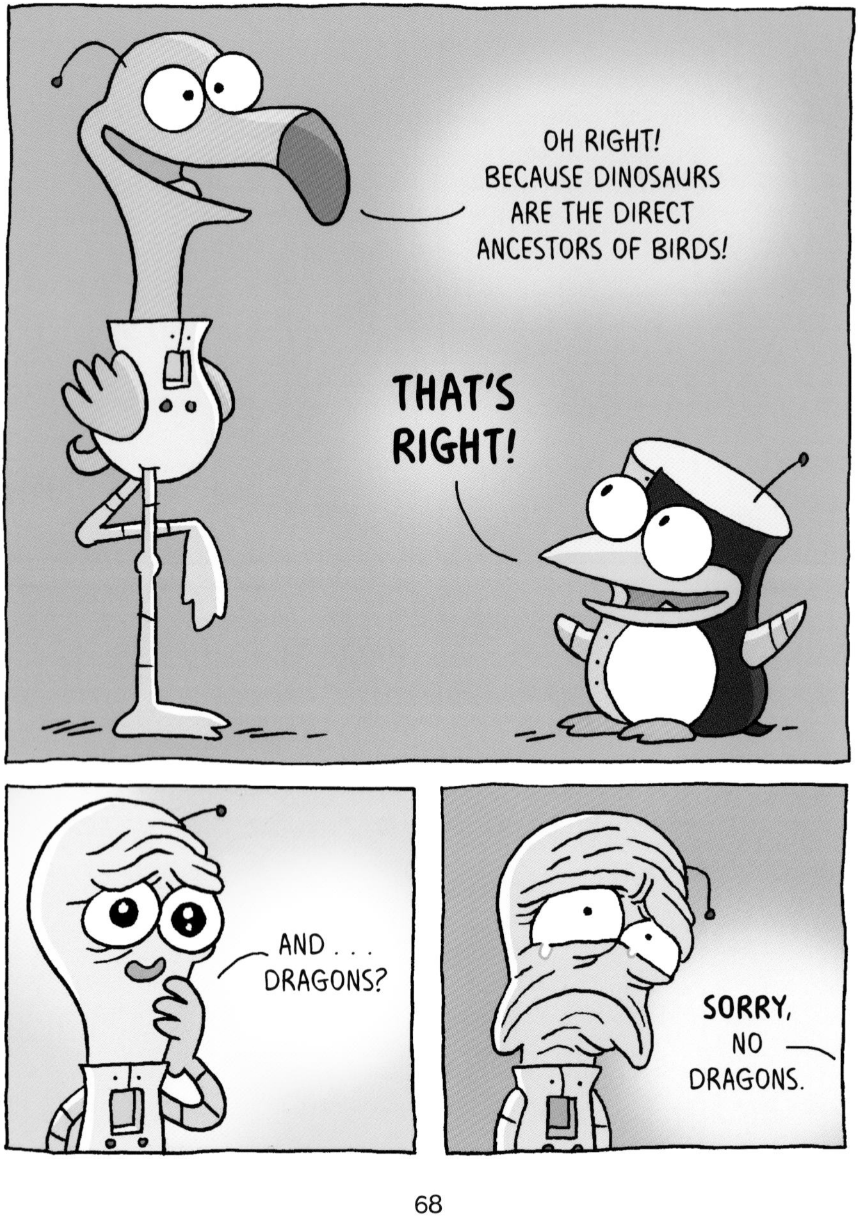
OH RIGHT! BECAUSE DINOSAURS ARE THE DIRECT ANCESTORS OF BIRDS!
THAT'S RIGHT!
AND . . . DRAGONS?
SORRY, NO DRAGONS.

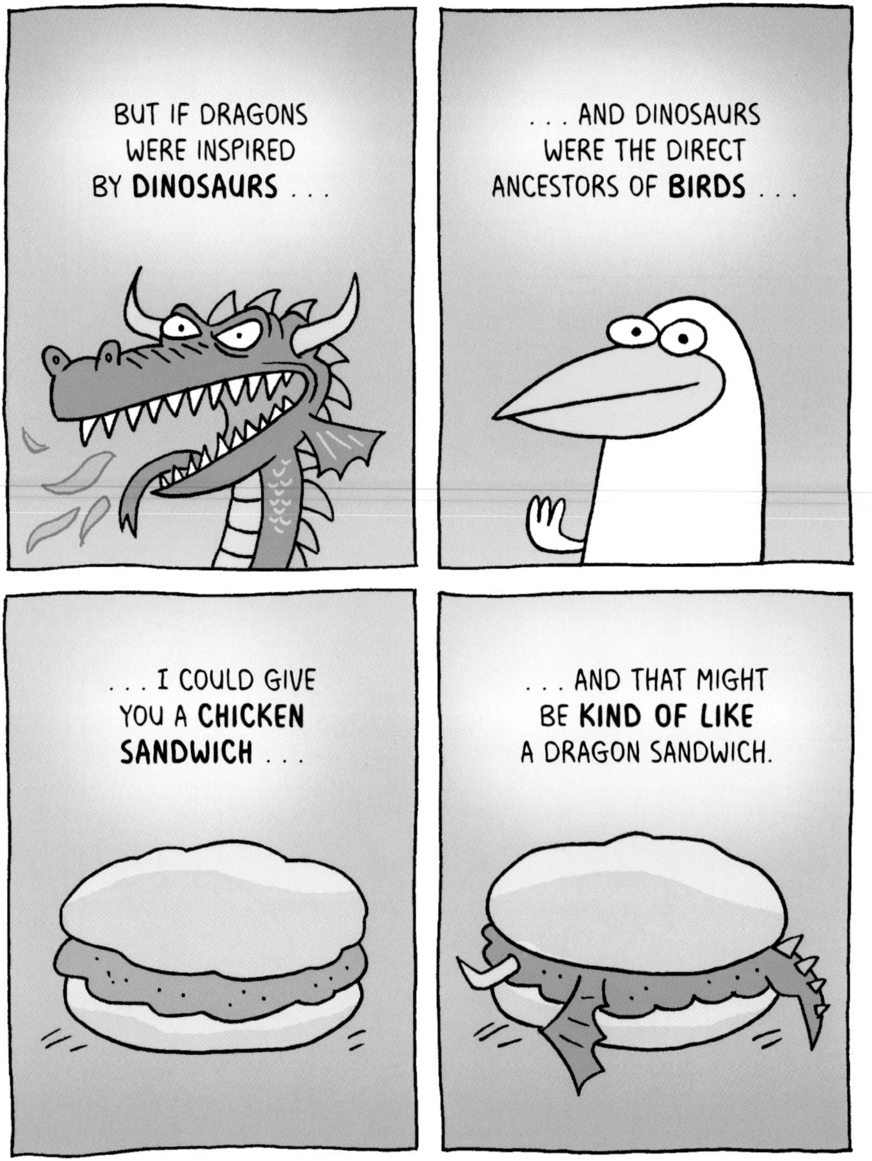
BUT IF DRAGONS WERE INSPIRED BY **DINOSAURS** . . .
. . . AND DINOSAURS WERE THE DIRECT ANCESTORS OF **BIRDS** . . .
. . . I COULD GIVE YOU A **CHICKEN SANDWICH** . . .
. . . AND THAT MIGHT BE **KIND OF LIKE** A DRAGON SANDWICH.

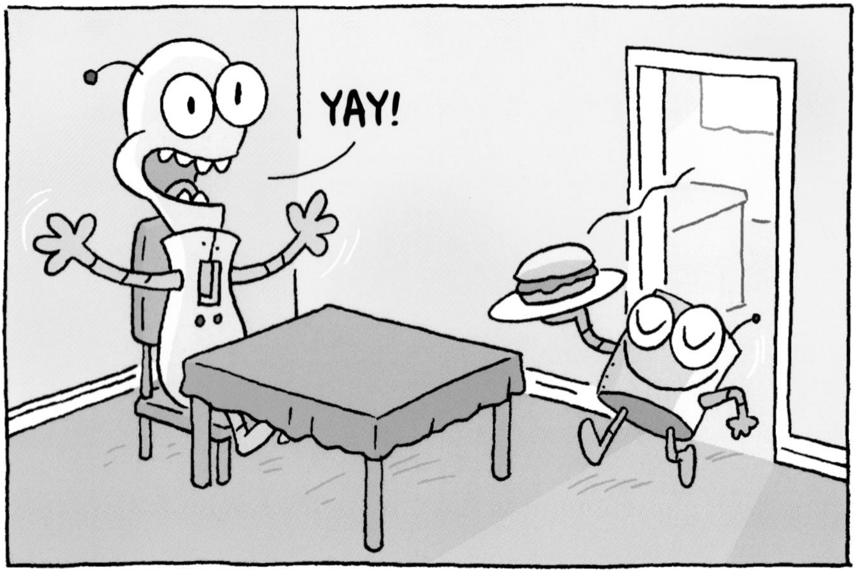
YAY!

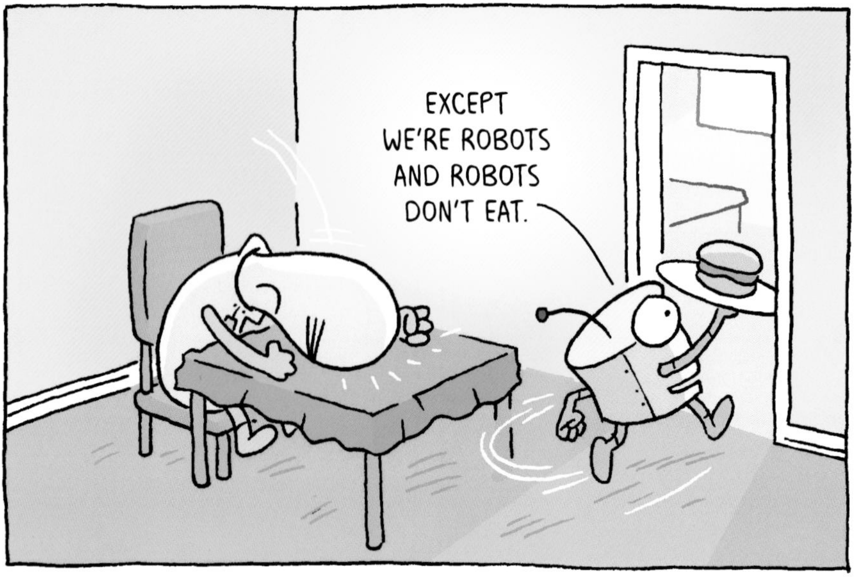
EXCEPT WE'RE ROBOTS AND ROBOTS DON'T EAT.

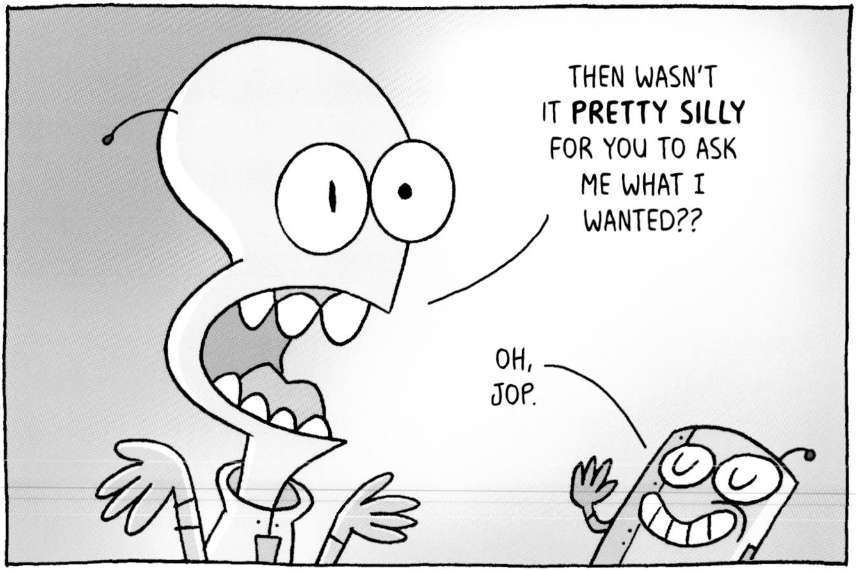
THEN WASN'T IT **PRETTY SILLY** FOR YOU TO ASK ME WHAT I WANTED??
OH, JOP.

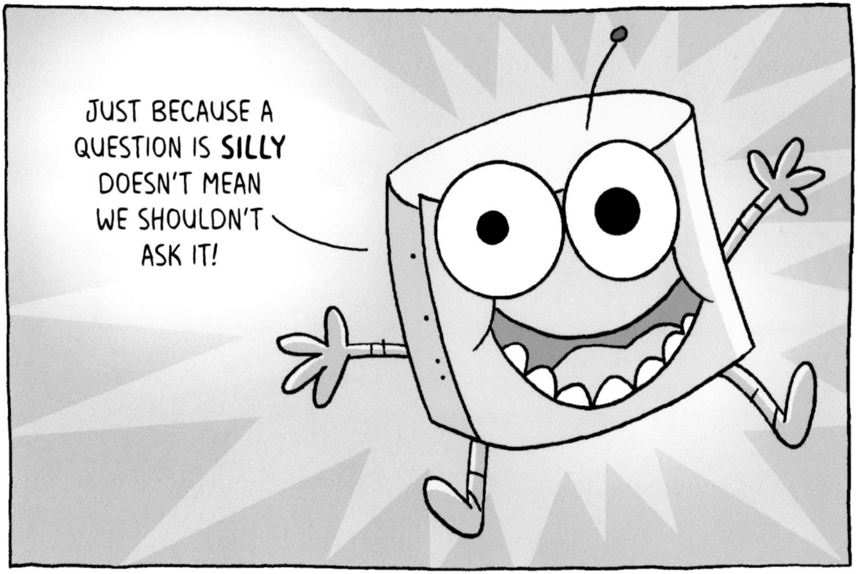
JUST BECAUSE A QUESTION IS **SILLY** DOESN'T MEAN WE SHOULDN'T ASK IT!

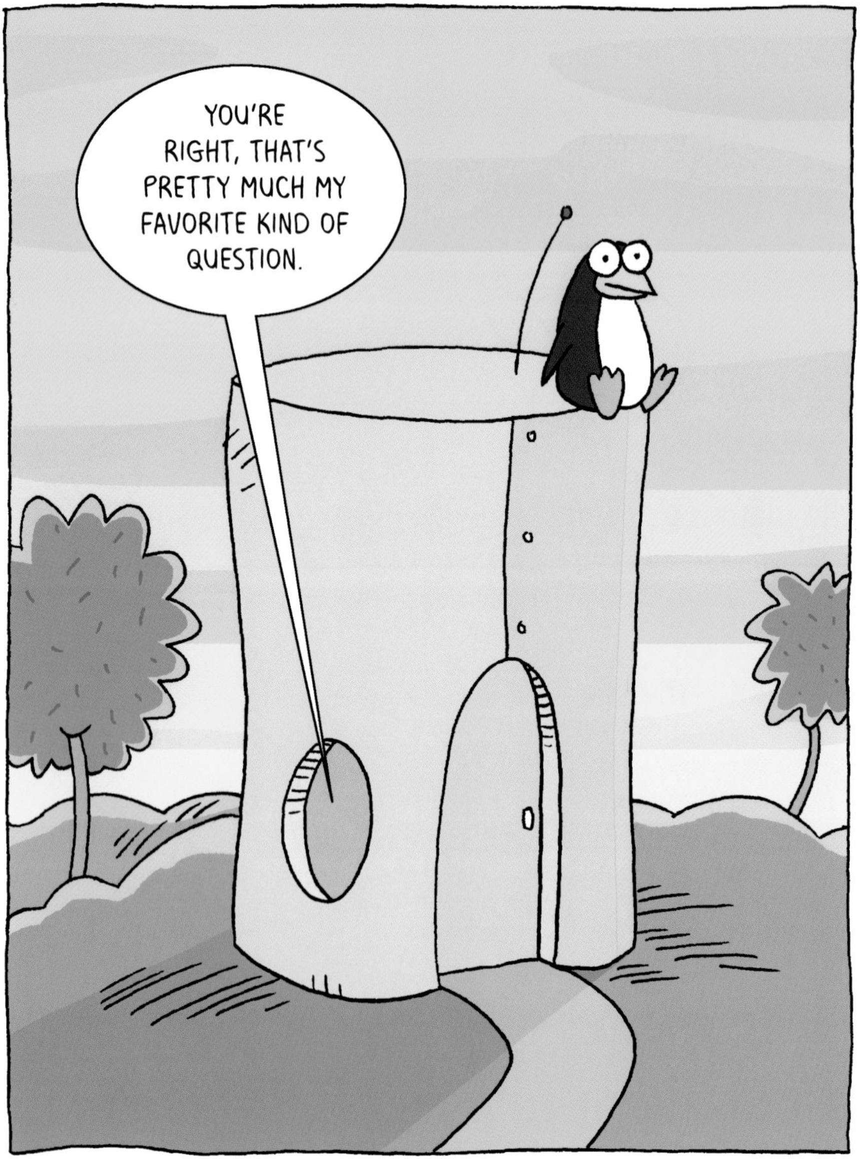
YOU'RE RIGHT, THAT'S PRETTY MUCH MY FAVORITE KIND OF QUESTION.

YOU KNOW THAT A DINOSAUR COULD BE ANY COLOR AND MIGHT HAVE HAD FEATHERS.

TRACE AND COLOR THIS ONE ANY WAY **YOU** WANT TO.

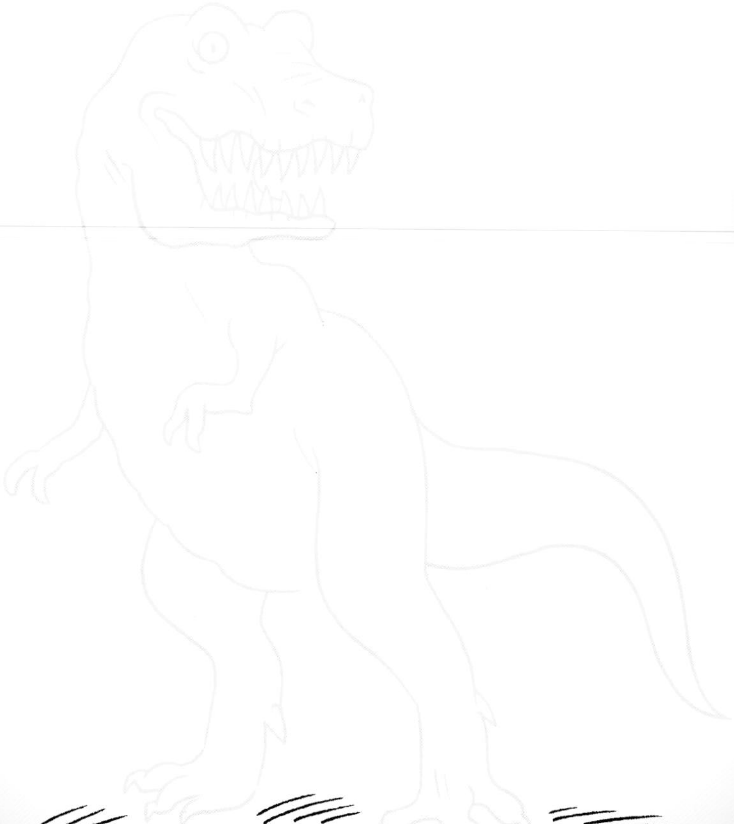

THE SENSORY SURPRISE

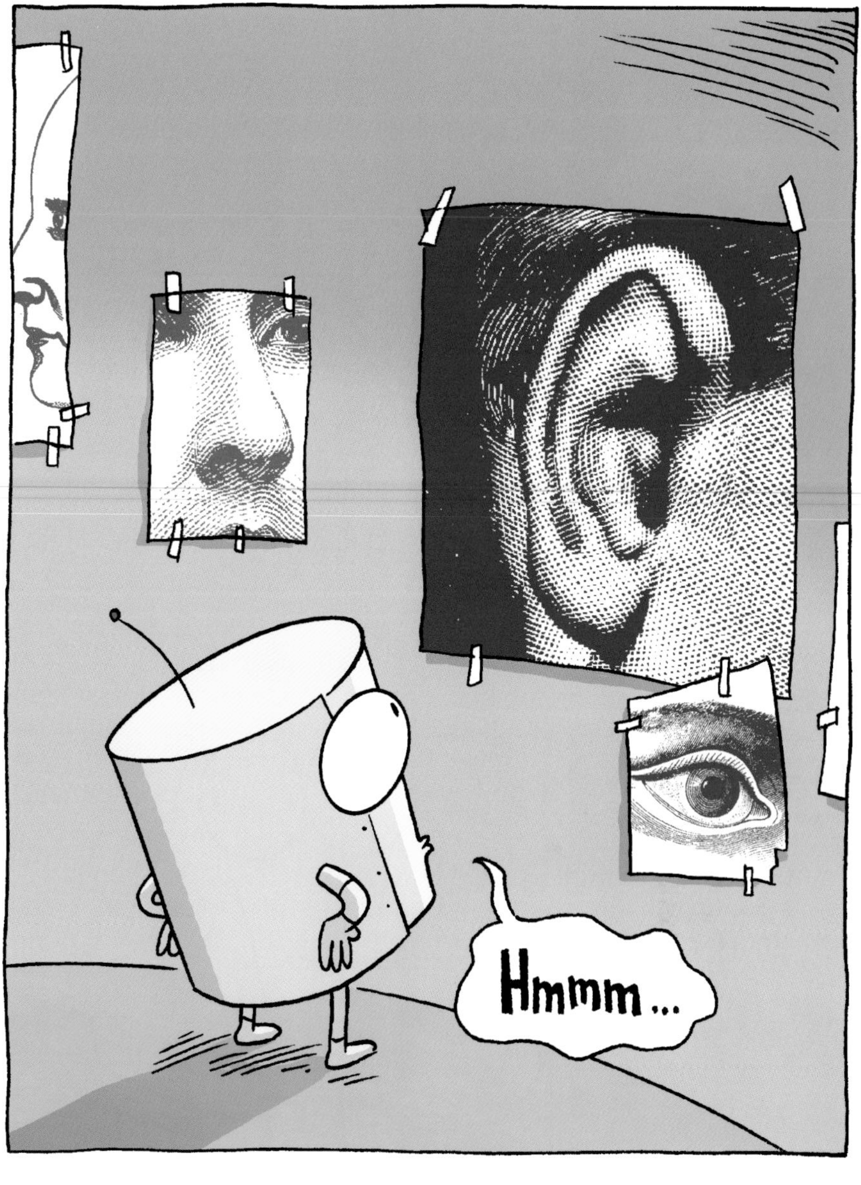
Hmmm...

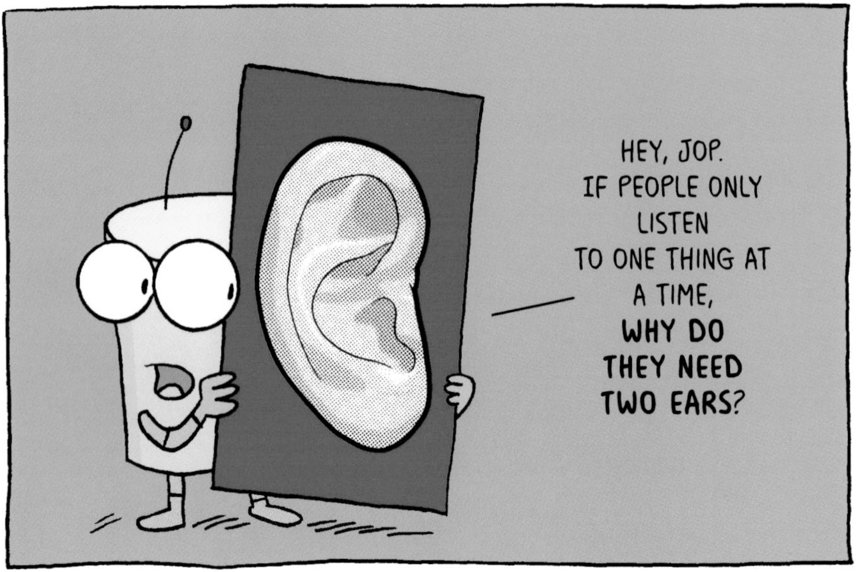
HEY, JOP.
IF PEOPLE ONLY LISTEN TO ONE THING AT A TIME, **WHY DO THEY NEED TWO EARS?**

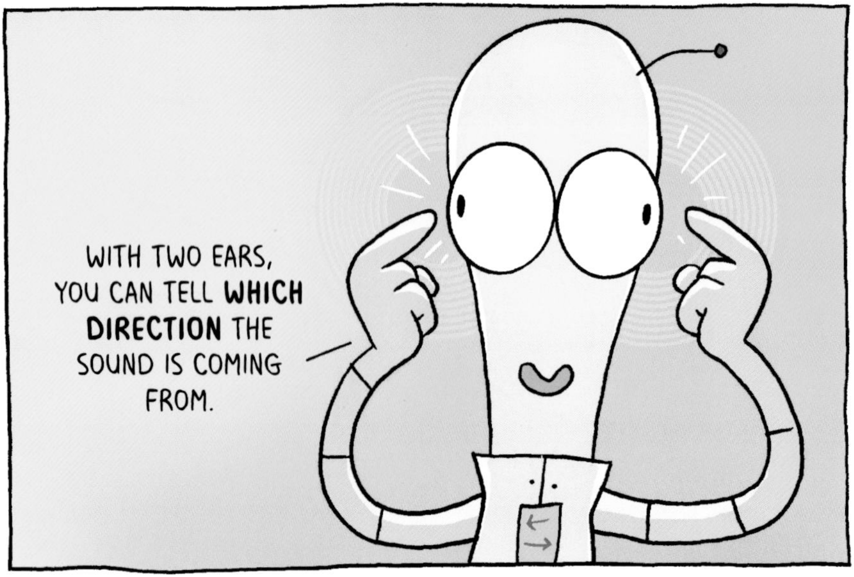
WITH TWO EARS, YOU CAN TELL **WHICH DIRECTION** THE SOUND IS COMING FROM.

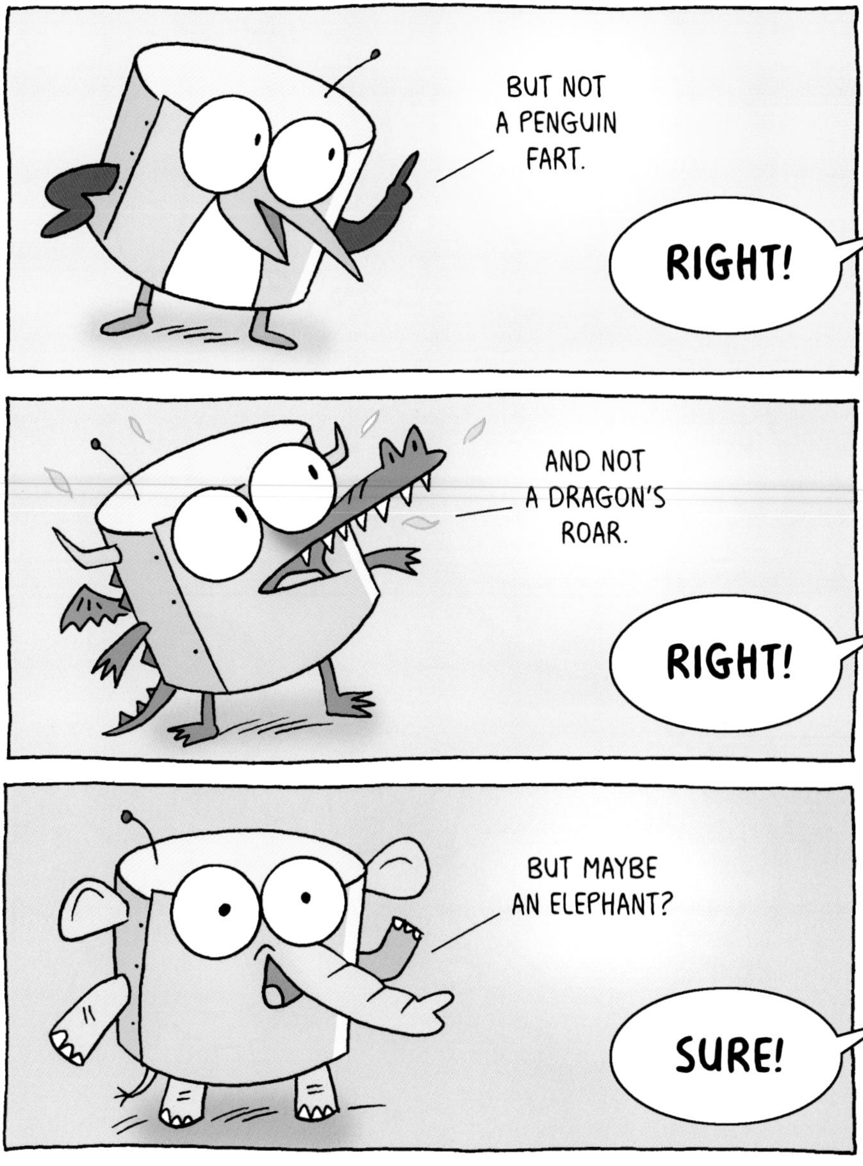
BUT NOT A PENGUIN FART.
RIGHT!
AND NOT A DRAGON'S ROAR.
RIGHT!
BUT MAYBE AN ELEPHANT?
SURE!

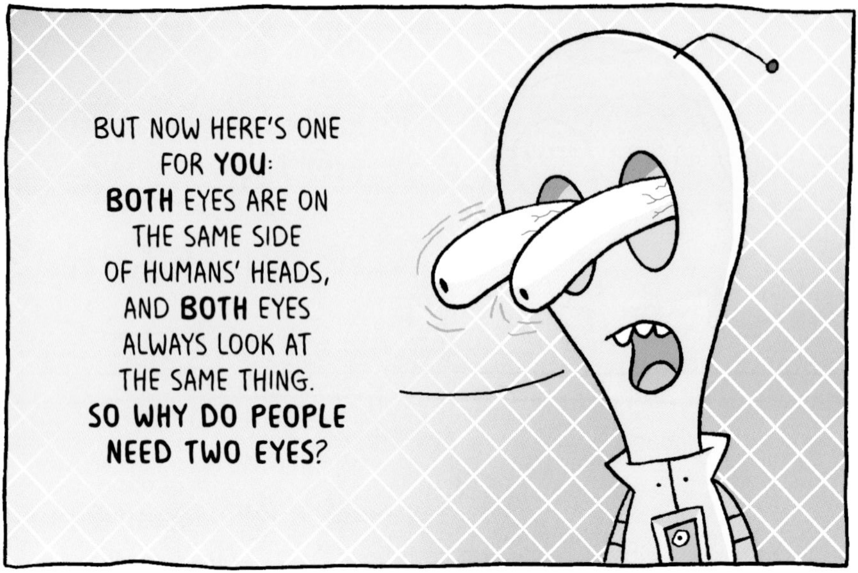
BUT NOW HERE'S ONE FOR **YOU**: **BOTH** EYES ARE ON THE SAME SIDE OF HUMANS' HEADS, AND **BOTH** EYES ALWAYS LOOK AT THE SAME THING. **SO WHY DO PEOPLE NEED TWO EYES?**

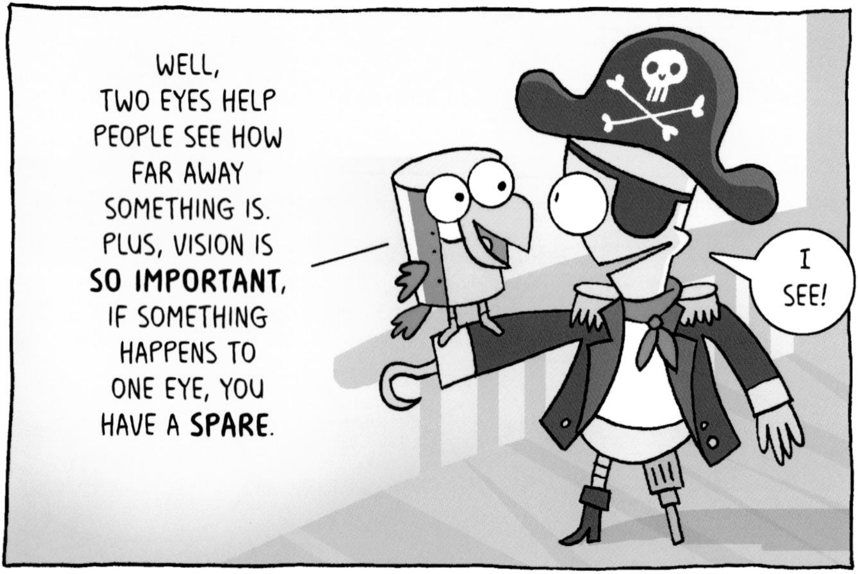
WELL, TWO EYES HELP PEOPLE SEE HOW FAR AWAY SOMETHING IS. PLUS, VISION IS **SO IMPORTANT**, IF SOMETHING HAPPENS TO ONE EYE, YOU HAVE A **SPARE**.
I SEE!

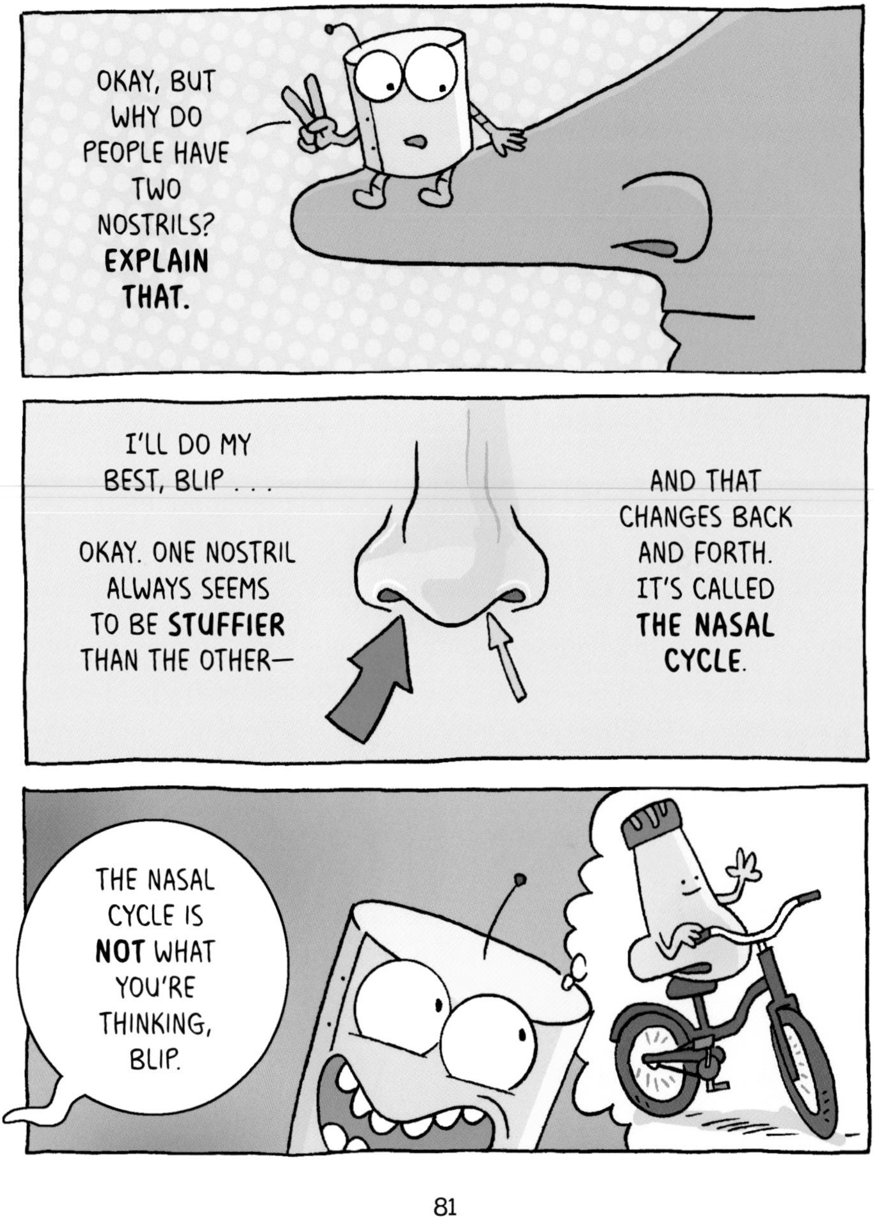
OKAY, BUT WHY DO PEOPLE HAVE TWO NOSTRILS? **EXPLAIN THAT.**
I'LL DO MY BEST, BLIP . . .
OKAY. ONE NOSTRIL ALWAYS SEEMS TO BE **STUFFIER** THAN THE OTHER—
AND THAT CHANGES BACK AND FORTH. IT'S CALLED **THE NASAL CYCLE**.
THE NASAL CYCLE IS **NOT** WHAT YOU'RE THINKING, BLIP.

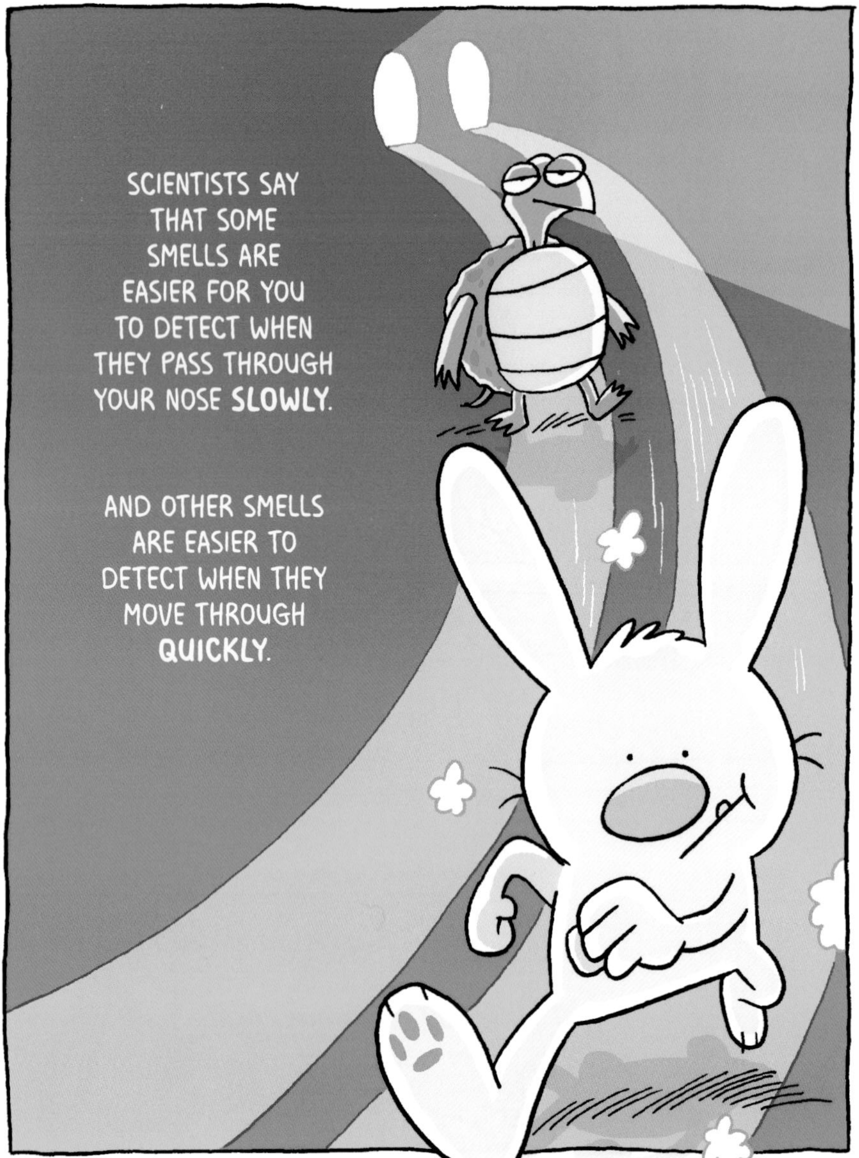
SCIENTISTS SAY THAT SOME SMELLS ARE EASIER FOR YOU TO DETECT WHEN THEY PASS THROUGH YOUR NOSE **SLOWLY**.
AND OTHER SMELLS ARE EASIER TO DETECT WHEN THEY MOVE THROUGH **QUICKLY**.

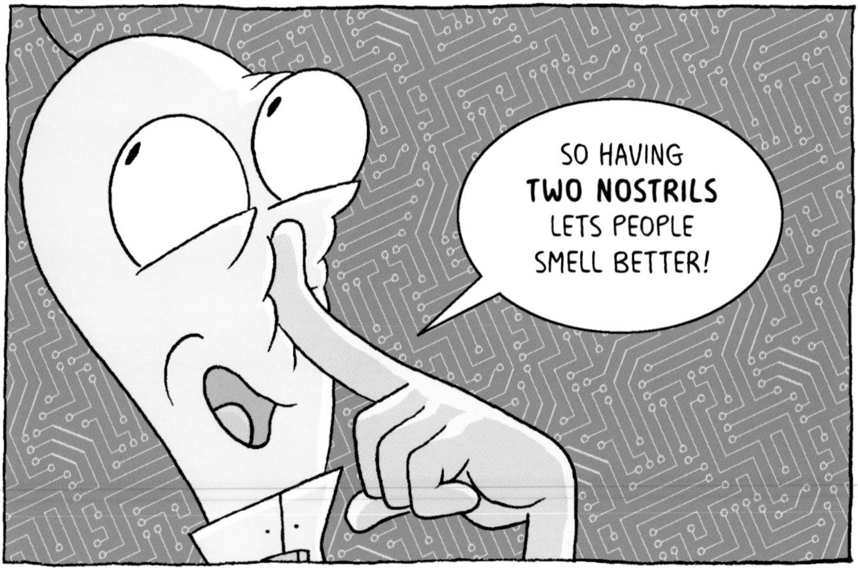
SO HAVING **TWO NOSTRILS** LETS PEOPLE SMELL BETTER!

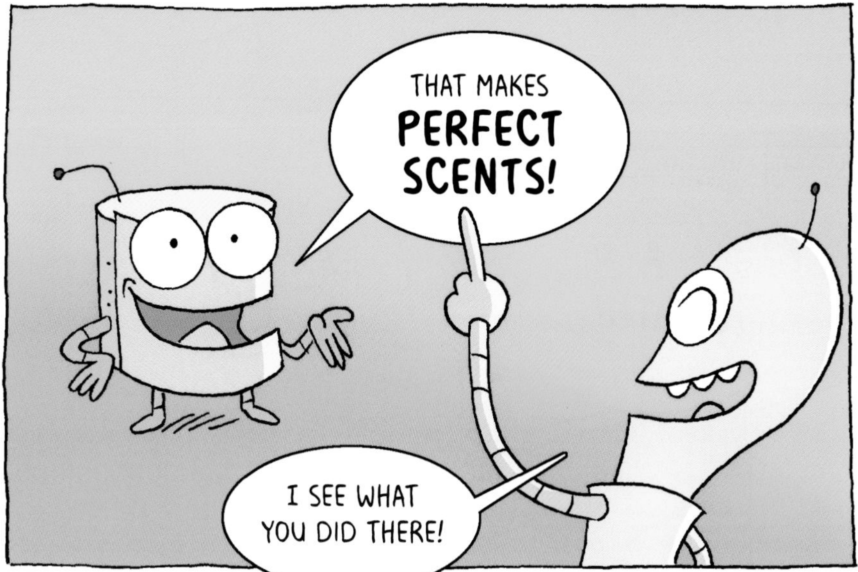
THAT MAKES **PERFECT SCENTS!**
I SEE WHAT YOU DID THERE!

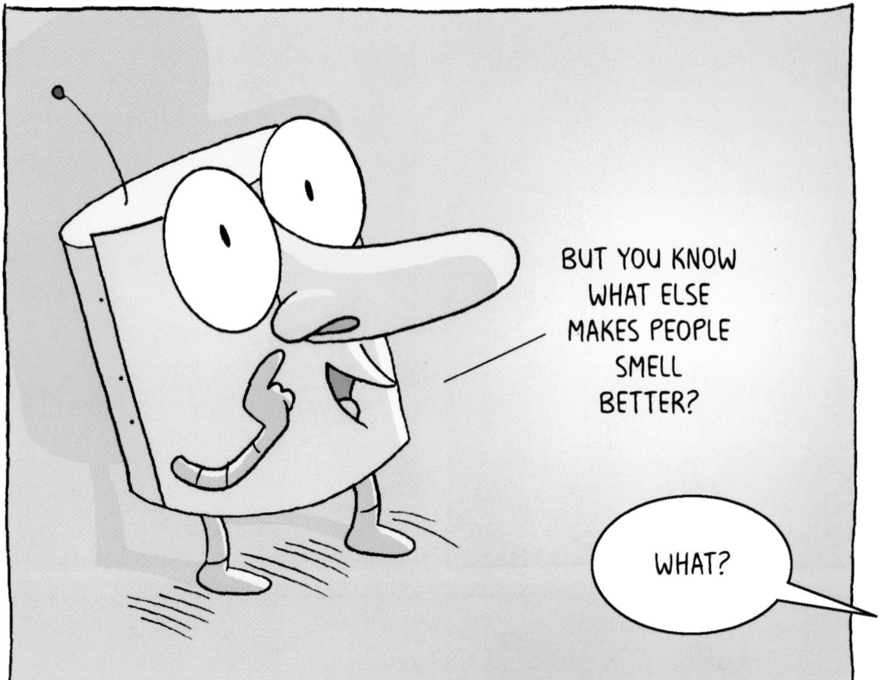
BUT YOU KNOW WHAT ELSE MAKES PEOPLE SMELL BETTER?
WHAT?

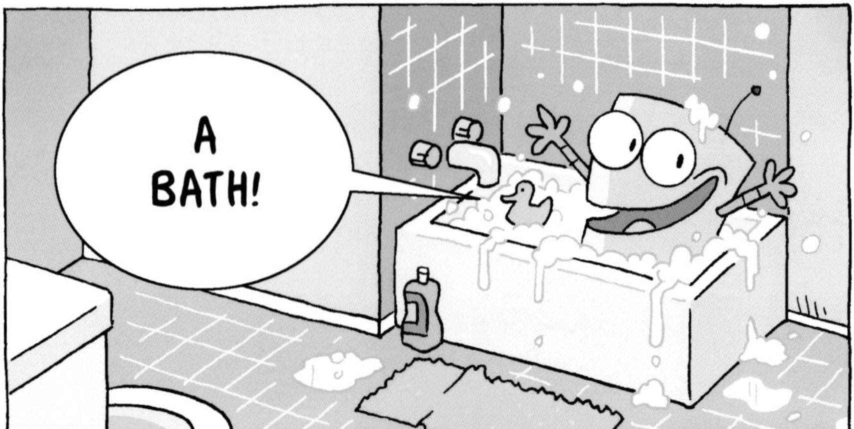
A BATH!

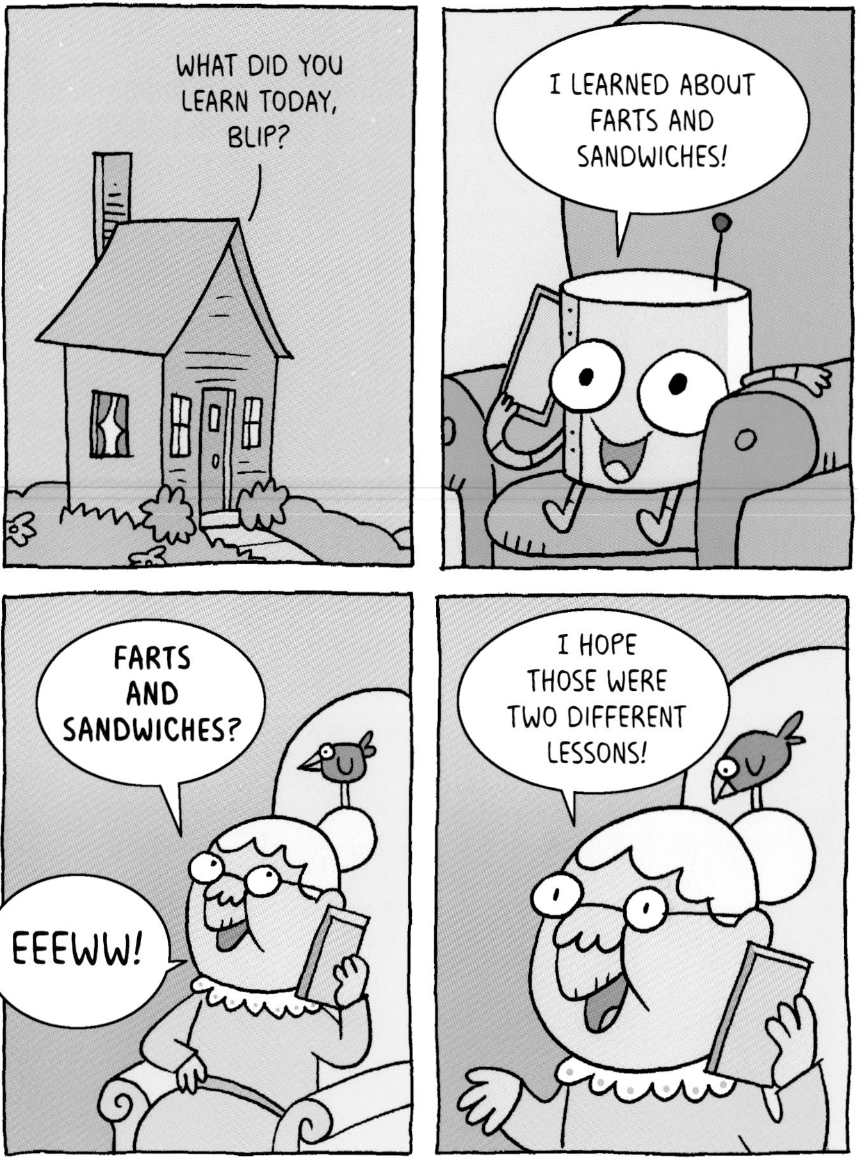

WHAT DID YOU LEARN TODAY, BLIP?
I LEARNED ABOUT FARTS AND SANDWICHES!
FARTS AND SANDWICHES?
EEEWW!
I HOPE THOSE WERE TWO DIFFERENT LESSONS!

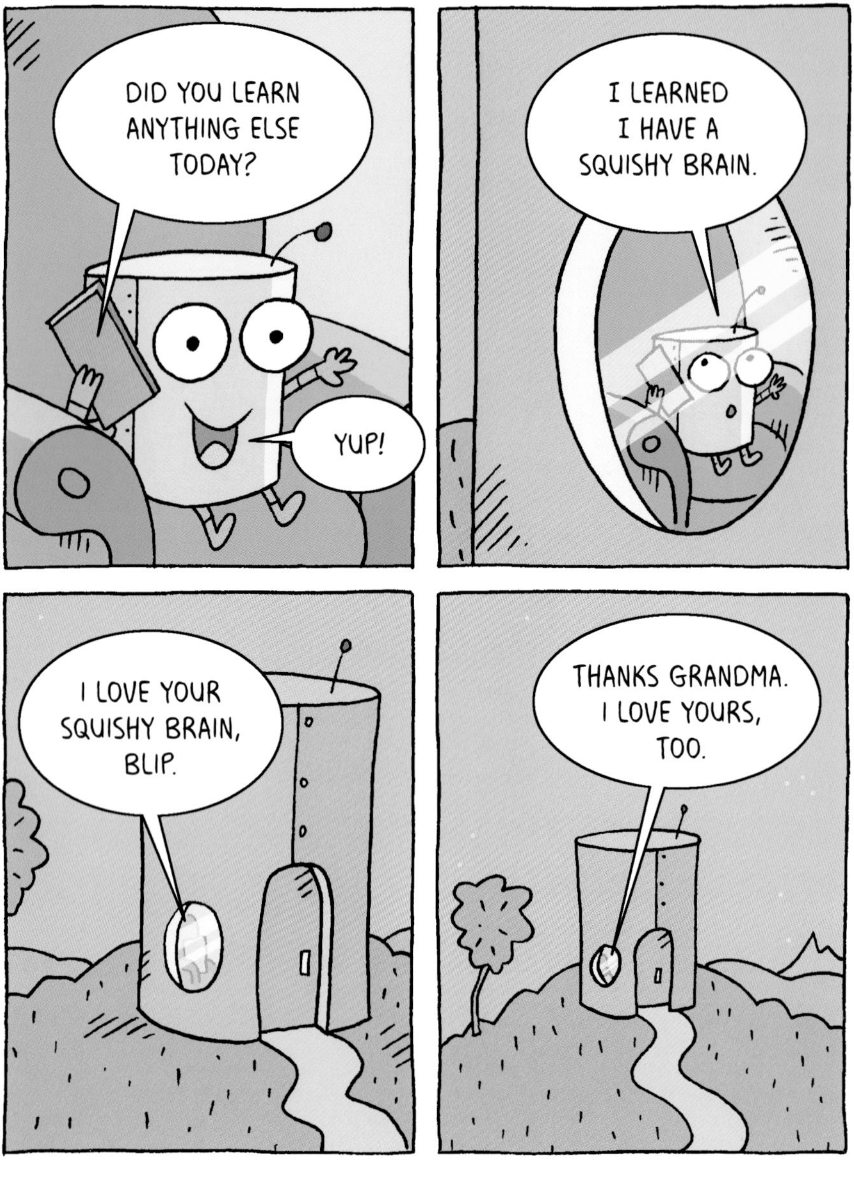
DID YOU LEARN ANYTHING ELSE TODAY?
YUP!
I LEARNED I HAVE A SQUISHY BRAIN.
I LOVE YOUR SQUISHY BRAIN, BLIP.
THANKS GRANDMA. I LOVE YOURS, TOO.

YOU KNOW THAT THIS IS NOTHING
LIKE THE INSIDE OF A PENGUIN,

BUT WE CAN PRETEND IT IS AND SEE IF YOU CAN FIGURE
OUT A PATH TO MOVE THE HOT DOG FROM BEGINNING TO END.

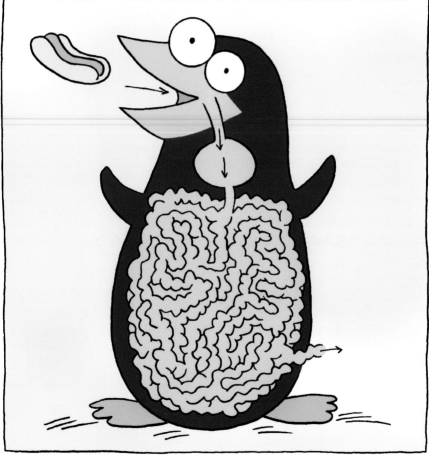

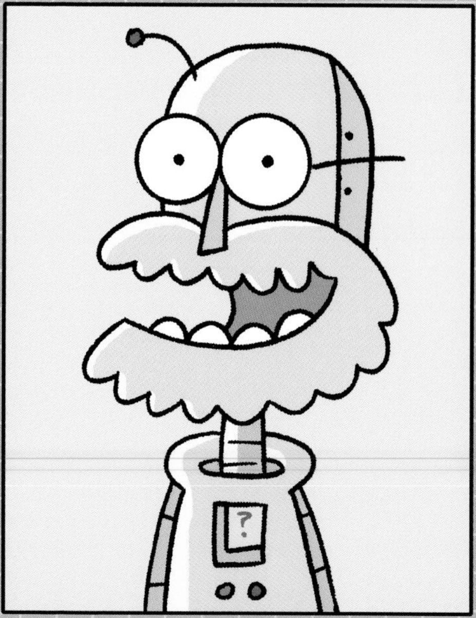

COURTESY OF THE AUTHOR

ABOUT THE AUTHOR

JIM BENTON IS THE AWARD-WINNING CREATOR OF THE *NEW YORK TIMES* BESTSELLING SERIES DEAR DUMB DIARY, FRANNY K. STEIN, CATWAD, *COMET THE UNSTOPPABLE REINDEER*, AND THE IT'S HAPPY BUNNY BRAND. HIS BOOKS HAVE SOLD MORE THAN FIFTEEN MILLION COPIES IN OVER A DOZEN LANGUAGES AND HAVE GARNERED NUMEROUS HONORS. LIKE JOP AND BLIP, HE ALSO ASKS WEIRD QUESTIONS ALL THE TIME.

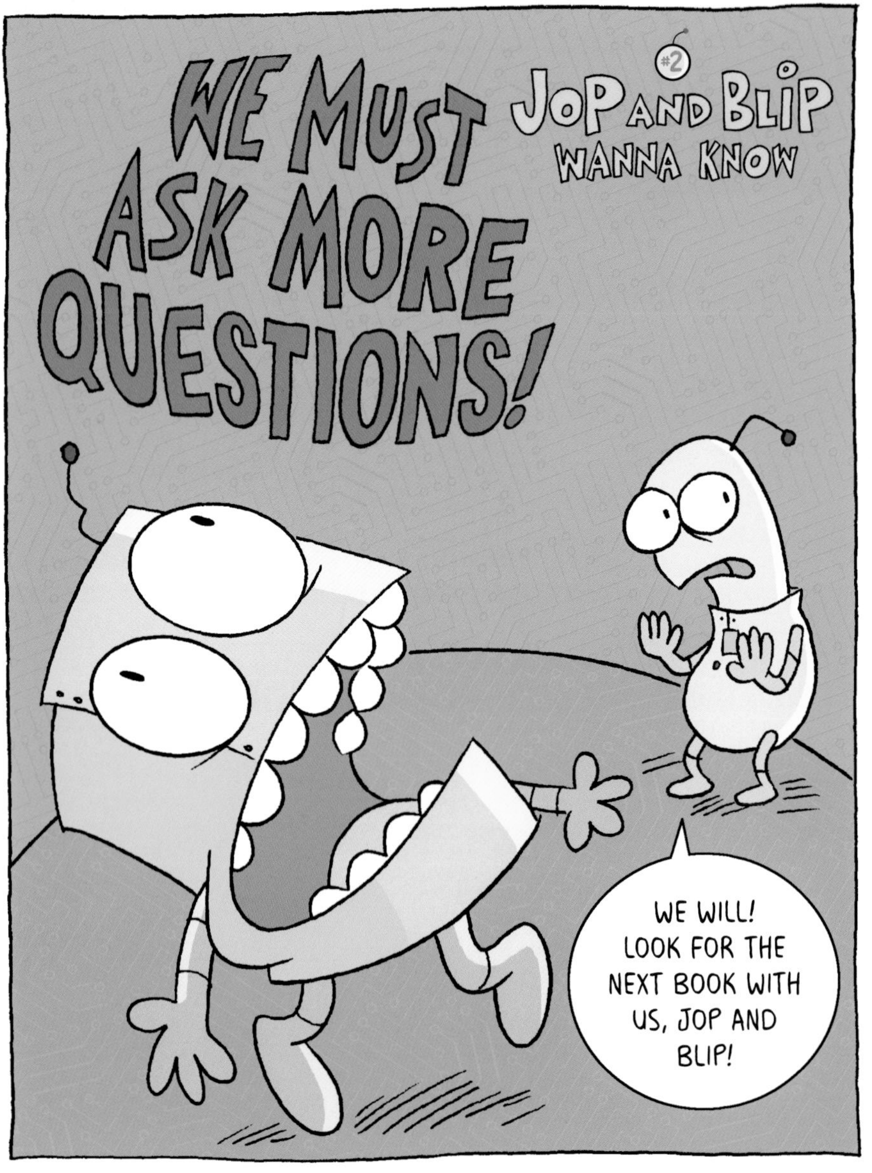
WE MUST ASK MORE QUESTIONS!
#2
JOP AND BLIP
WANNA KNOW
WE WILL! LOOK FOR THE NEXT BOOK WITH US, JOP AND BLIP!